The Poodle Problem

The Poodle Problem

Anna Wilson

Illustrated by Clare Elsom

MACMILLAN CHILDREN'S BOOKS

First published 2012 by Macmillan Children's Books
an imprint of Pan Macmillan, a division of Macmillan Publishers Limited
Pan Macmillan, 20 New Wharf Road, London N1 9RR
Basingstoke and Oxford
Associated companies throughout the world
www.panmacmillan.com

ISBN 978-0-330-54527-3

Text copyright © Anna Wilson 2012
Illustrations copyright © Clare Elsom 2012

5 7 9 8 6 4

A CIP catalogue record for this book is available from
the British Library.

Printed and bound by CPI Group (UK) Ltd, Croydon CR0 4YY

For Rachel, Emma, Tanya and Harriet at
The Courtyard Hair & Beauty, without whom the
Pooch Parlour idea would never have been born

The Introductory Bit

This is the story of a small (and rather handsome) dog.

That'll be me she's talking about.

Yes. You don't need to be *quite* so conceited though, do you?

Sorry about that. As I was saying. This is the story of a small dog and how he solved a large (and rather tricky) mystery. His name is – no, I shan't tell you his name yet. That would spoil things, and we can't have that. You'll have to read on to find out what his name is, as he doesn't appear until later. I can, however, tell you the name of the lovely lady he came to live with, because she is in this story right from the beginning, so that won't spoil anything at all. Now you'd better stop fidgeting, because we're ready to begin.

Welcome to Crumbly-under-Edge!

Mrs Fudge was the lovely old lady in question. She had snowy-white hair and a jolly face and her full name was Semolina Ribena Fudge, which I'm sure you'll agree is quite an awkward name, and it's true that she wasn't overly fond of it. She didn't mind the 'Fudge' bit as that had been her late husband's surname. (I say he was her 'late husband', not because he was never on time for anything, but because, sadly, he was dead by the time this story starts.)

He was a wonderful man, dears (if a little bossy at times).

Mr and Mrs Fudge had travelled the world together – and the Seven Seas. They'd fought pirates and swum with dolphins. But after many years of adventure they decided it was time to settle down. And that is how they came to buy their large, rambling house in Liquorice Drive in the country town of Crumbly-under-Edge.

Crumbly-under-Edge was a sleepy, pretty little place. It had a main street with a few shops. And it had some windy, cobbledy not-so-main streets with houses painted pleasing shades of blue and pink and green and creamy white so that, from a distance, they looked like rows of marshmallows or iced buns. The houses and shops were very well looked after.

By the time you come to meet her, dear reader, Mrs Fudge had been living in the town for years and years and eons and indeed yonks (which is a technical term for a very long time indeed). She was quite happy – however she did feel the house was rather too big for one old person. And never having approved of waste of any kind (especially a waste of space), Mrs Fudge thought *maybe* she should open up part of her house for the purposes of running a little business. So, after much thought and planning, she came up with the idea of turning part of the ground floor of the house into a hairdressing salon called 'Chop 'n' Chat'.

There's always ladies wanting their hair done.

And how right she was about that! Chop 'n' Chat was soon a *booming* business, for not only was Mrs Fudge a marvellous hairdresser, she was also a very good listener and made the best cup of tea and the lightest fluffiest sponge cake this side of the Atlantic Ocean (I can't speak for the other side, not having been there myself at the time of writing).

So Mrs Fudge had arranged her life so that it

was just about perfect, you might say . . . There
was one thing though: even though Mrs Fudge
had many, many customers who kept her busy, and
even though she had a particularly gorgeous fluffy
grey cat called Muffles, and even though she *loved*
her town and her house and her baking, Mrs Fudge
could get lonely sometimes.

And this was a thought that kept her up at night
occasionally and made the long winter evenings seem
even longer and more wintery than they actually
were. It became clear to Mrs Fudge that she had to do
something about this. And so she pondered . . .

And that's where
I come in.

Yes, thank you, Pippa . . .
(It would be nice if
people didn't *insist*
on interrupting
me.)

Pippa Peppercorn was a girl (obviously) who was ten and a quarter, and didn't mind who knew it. In fact, she was exceedingly proud of the quartery bit, as it meant she was well on her way to becoming eleven (which is, as everyone knows, almost fully grown-up). She had very few friends her own age, mainly because she felt that most other ten-and-a-quarter-year-olds were only interested in sleepover parties and giggling, whereas *she* had her eye firmly fixed on the future.

And, as it happened, Mrs Fudge was of the opinion that most other extremely old people were rather dull and only liked sucking toffees and saying, 'It wouldn't happen in my day.' So when Pippa walked into Chop 'n' Chat one day with a sulk that could have sunk a thousand ships and muttered, 'Teacher says I have to get my hair cut,' and Mrs Fudge smiled in an understanding way and said, 'Would you like an apricot flapjack?' a lifelong friendship was born.

Now we've got all that straight, I think we should get on with the story.

What about me?

I've already explained: you come in later.

But—

I've got to set the scene, haven't I?

But—!

Who's telling this story?

sulks

2

Pippa Peppercorn Comes to the Rescue

In the usual run of things, you would expect that
a girl of ten and a quarter would have to ask her
parents' permission to take on a Saturday job. But
luckily for Pippa (and for this story) we don't have
to worry about all that. Pippa's parents were always
busy, and when they heard that the wonderful Mrs
Fudge was giving their daughter something to do at
the weekend they were so over the moon that they
could have written to the Association of Astronauts
to tell them what the dark side of it looked like.
(Dark, presumably.)

'That is a lovely idea,' said Mr Peppercorn, not
looking up from his newspaper.

'Make sure Mrs Fudge gives you the recipe for her

sponge cake, won't you?' said Mrs Peppercorn, not looking up from her book.

And you won't hear much more from Pippa Peppercorn's parents, because frankly they were such a tedious pair it would bore you rigid.

Pippa found herself counting down the days, hours, minutes and seconds until that first Saturday morning arrived. And since counting every second of every day takes rather a lot of concentration Pippa missed out on a few things, such as people asking her to partner them for table tennis or go to the cinema with them. But Pippa didn't notice. She was too busy counting.

The Saturday of Pippa's new job finally dawned. But Pippa was up well before the dawn. She was up while it was as dark as the darkest cave. And to top it all, her bedside light wasn't working, so she fell out of bed and had to fumble around for her slippers and a torch, which luckily she always kept under the bed in case of burglars. She thought that if a burglar was ever cheeky enough to come into her room in the dark, she could grab her torch, shine it in his face to bedazzle the daylights out of him and then make a run for it.

She found the torch, turned it on and got dressed. Then she crept downstairs and made herself some pancakes and fried some bacon and boiled the kettle for a cup of tea. Pippa was quite handy like that.

But even after she'd done all those things, the kitchen clock insisted that it was only seven o'clock.

'Oh, blow it!' Pippa told the clock. 'Couldn't you

11

please move a little bit faster? I'm going to have to give the kitchen a good old clean now to pass the time.'

The clock unfortunately did not react to being told off, even when Pippa gave it her hardest glare, so she put her hands on her skinny hips, sighed a big loud snorty sigh and looked around her to decide where to start on her cleaning.

The kitchen was not very dirty or messy, so she decided to pass the time by rearranging things instead of cleaning them. She became so absorbed in moving chairs and jugs and plates and bowls and pots and pans that, without her noticing, the kitchen clock eventually *did* get a move on and all of a sudden (or so it seemed), it was . . .

'HALF PAST EIGHT!' Pippa shouted, punching the air in a victory salute, narrowly missing the rather beautiful pyramid she had made of all the cups and saucers in the house.

She ran to the hall, took her red duffel coat from its peg, grabbed her black woolly hat and, checking

she had her keys, let herself out into the cold autumn morning.

Mrs Fudge too was awake before the dawn had leaked around the edges of the sky. She found that the older she got, the less sleep she tended to need, and so she was often up at a time most normal people would be cosily tucked up in bed. This meant that she had lots of extra time in her day for doing all the things she had been too busy to do when she was younger, namely baking, learning the banjo and knitting. (Sometimes she even knitted little cakes to use as cheery decorations.)

And so, even though it was incredibly early and still rather dark outside, Mrs Fudge was up and about. She had neatly brushed and combed her hair, and she was wearing a fresh dress (her favourite one, with the red and pink swirls) with a blue flowery apron over it to keep herself clean. She was humming a little song of her own devising and tidying her kitchen and baking some scones. The wind howled outside, sending flurries of leaves leaping and whirling against the windows, but Mrs Fudge's kitchen was invitingly snug and warm.

'I must make the place look extra-specially cosy and nice for young Pippa's first day,' she said, as she shined the taps on the sink.

She wasn't talking to herself, I should add. She was talking to her cat, Muffles. Muffles wasn't paying

14

attention though. She was licking her bottom, as cats have a habit of doing when you are talking to them. It's rude and ungracious of them, I agree, but what can you do? A cat will always lick its bottom if it possibly can.

which is why DOGS are so much more sophisticated.

Mrs Fudge tutted (as indeed I will do to a CERTAIN DOG in a minute), sighed and went back to tidying the kitchen until the timer went PING! which meant the scones were ready. She fetched a stripy oven glove and bent to open the oven door. As she did so, a warm, golden crumbly smell of good fresh baking filled the room. Mrs Fudge closed her eyes, the better to appreciate the aroma, and smiled.

'Enough for all my customers this morning,' she said appreciatively, opening her eyes again and setting the scones down on a wire rack to cool.

The sun was peeking in through the crack in the curtains by now, the wind had calmed its bad temper and the kettle had just boiled. Muffles opened one eye to check that everything was as it should be, saw that it was, and closed it again. Mrs Fudge made herself a nice pot of tea and sank down into her favourite armchair by the window to have five minutes' peace before her day began.

3

A Second Breakfast

'I wonder if I'll get to do any actual cutting of hair,' said Pippa to herself as she skipped along the rain-streaked lanes.

She kicked at a mound of soggy leaves with her red-booted foot and sent them sliding muddily across the path.

'I would LOVE to get to do some snip-snip-snippety-snipping!' she cried, jumping in a puddle and making great slashing movements with her blue-gloved fingers.

She broke into a run as she turned on to Liquorice Drive. Her incredibly long red plaits bounced jerkily on her shoulders and flapped in her face, and her black woolly hat slipped ever so slightly down over her turquoise eyes. But she was so fizz-poppingly full of excitement that she didn't notice.

Everything about this Saturday was going to be wonderful, Pippa was certain. Even Mrs Fudge's house seemed to smile at Pippa as she ran to the front door. She squealed and clasped her hands together at the thought of being allowed to really truly work there. Then she took a deep breath to stop herself from squealing any more.

'I have a job now,' she told herself. 'I must be grown-up and sensible.'

She reached up a blue woolly finger to ring the doorbell. The door opened immediately, bathing Pippa in warmth and light.

'My dear!' said Mrs Fudge, standing back from the door and gesturing to Pippa to come in. 'Welcome to your first day at Chop 'n' Chat!'

Pippa wiped her wellied feet enthusiastically on the doormat, entered the house and took her boots off, leaving them neatly side by side in the hall. Mrs Fudge took her coat and hat and showed

 18

her where to hang everything.

'That will be your first job,' she said. 'To take coats and hats from customers, hang them up and return them when people leave.'

'OK, and then do I get to do some snipping?' said Pippa eagerly.

Mrs Fudge raised one eyebrow in alarm and said quickly, 'I wonder if you've already had breakfast. Well, it doesn't matter if you have. They say breakfast is the most important meal of the day, so it stands to reason you can't have too many breakfasts. Come and have a scone, why don't you?'

Pippa didn't need to be asked twice. The very idea of a scone was even more appealing than the idea of snipping away with a huge pair of scissors.

'That is THE most gorgeously scrumptulicious baking smell I have ever smelt!' she cried as she followed the old lady into the kitchen and shrugged off her red woolly cardy.

Mrs Fudge gestured to the rocking chair by the stove. 'You sit there and warm your cockles, my dear,' she said, and handed Pippa a plate with a scone piled high with a glistening jewel of strawberry jam and a fluffy white cloud of cream.

Pippa's eyes opened to twice their normal size and flashed greedily as she took a bite of the delicious little cake and felt the sweet flavour fill her mouth.

Ten creamy minutes later Mrs Fudge led Pippa through to the salon and showed her where everything was kept. Muffles trotted behind, but kept her distance from Pippa's gangly legs which had a habit of going every which way as she skipped along.

Mrs Fudge then spent a few minutes showing Pippa how to fold the pretty coloured towels so that the ends were tucked away out of sight, how to clean the hairbrushes and how to sweep up the clippings from the floor once a customer had gone. Lastly she showed Pippa the scissors. Fixing her with a very serious look over the top of her half-moon spectacles she said, 'But only *I* shall be touching those. They are VERY sharp. Do you understand, Pippa dear?'

Pippa swallowed her disappointment. 'Yes,' she said sullenly.

'Good,' Mrs Fudge said brightly. Then she drew her husband's gold pocket watch from out of her apron (he had been given it by a particularly friendly pirate during their travels across the Seven Seas) and gasped. 'Mercy! Half past nine already. Marble Wainwright will be here in a matter of seconds.'

Muffles narrowed her eyes, flattened her ears and let out a low growl.

Pippa grimaced.

Mrs Fudge smiled weakly.

You see, although Mrs Fudge liked all her customers and rarely had a bad word to say about any of them, of all the people she had ever met, Marble Wainwright was one of the trickiest. It wasn't so much that she was rude or objectionable, although she could be both of these; it was more that she was prickly. And by that I don't mean that when you touched her you got a sharp pain in your fingers: I mean that she was irritable and easily offended.

'I wish somebody *else* could do Marble Wainwright's hair,' sighed Pippa. 'She is *such* a pain!'

'Miaow,' said Muffles, wrinkling her pretty pink nose.

'Now, now,' Mrs Fudge said gently. 'Chop 'n' Chat Rule Number One: even if our customer is a moaning Minnie, *we* are *not*.'

Pippa blushed. 'S'pose so,' she mumbled.

'Chop 'n' Chat Rule Number Two,' Mrs Fudge continued. 'Never wish our customers away to another hair salon! I don't want to be losing my clientele, thank you very much, however difficult, er, *unusual* they are,' she corrected herself hastily. 'Anyway, she always brings Snooks with her,' she added. 'And Snooks is a dear.'

Snooks was a scruffy little Welsh terrier, a friendly dog who loved being made a fuss of. He was the only thing that was nice about Marble. In fact, it was quite remarkable that someone as disagreeable as Marble could have such a delightful pet as Snooks. But luckily for Pippa (and for this story), she did. And you are just about to meet him.

Talking of dear and delightful dogs . . . Oh, for the love of cupcakes! DO be quiet and wait your turn.

4

A Difficult Customer

'Now, Pippa dear, I should warn you that Marble can be a little, er, shall we say, *adventurous* in her hair-styling requests,' Mrs Fudge said gently.

Pippa spluttered. 'Everyone knows that!' she exclaimed. 'You only have to *look* at her to see that!'

Marble came to Chop 'n' Chat at least once a month, and she always brought a scrapbook containing pictures she had cut out from magazines and newspapers. She would open the scrapbook on her chosen page, thrust it into Mrs Fudge's hand and rudely make the same demand: 'I want to look like *this*!'

Now even Pippa (who had never had a job in a hair salon before) understood this simple fact: if you

24

don't look like a film star *before* you enter a hair salon, you are quite unlikely to look like one when you leave.

Don't get me wrong, Mrs Fudge was a tippity-top hairdresser. She always made her customers look fresh and tidy and far more presentable than when they first sat down in one of her twirly-whirly chairs. But it is a fact of nature that you have what you are born with and you have to make the best of it. Marble, however, had ideas above and beyond what nature had given her.

Every day she looked in the mirror with a sigh and a groan and set about flicking through magazines, books and newspapers with a view to finding the New Her. She scoured the pictures of celebrities and the images of royalty, she pored over the snapshots of supermodels and the glossy photo shoots of beauty queens, and the minute she found a picture that tickled her fancy, she would whip out her scissors, cut out the image and fix it securely with glue into her scrapbook.

'Marble is, erm, a *special* customer,' said Mrs Fudge to Pippa. 'She would like nothing better than to leave here resembling one of the Jollywood starlets in those magazines of hers. I do my best, but I worry that Marble thinks my best is not good enough. I can do anything to her *hair*, but . . .' She tailed off, sighing.

'You can't change her face.' Pippa took up the thread eagerly. 'Or her moodiness,' she added. 'Or her dress sense, or her frown, or her tone of voice, or—'

'Quite,' said Mrs Fudge. And she peered rather sternly over the top of her half-moon spectacles, making it clear that Pippa should watch her tongue. It was a ploy which had worked well with the late Mr Fudge, and it worked on Pippa now.

'Am I interrupting something?' said a sarcastic voice.

'Marble!' cried Mrs Fudge, her hands flying to her chest. 'My, you gave me a fright. I didn't hear the doorbell, my dear.'

 26

'That's because it doesn't work,' Marble grumbled.

Pippa opened her mouth to protest that it had been working half an hour ago, but Mrs Fudge was looking at her over the top of her specs again, so she closed her mouth and shrugged.

'Pippa, take Marble's hat and coat, won't you? And then perhaps you could hold on to Snooks for a second while I get Marble settled.'

Pippa wondered if Marble would ever get around to saying, 'Good morning,' or asking how she and Mrs Fudge were today. But the miserable old trout merely handed Pippa Snooks's lead and pulled off her own floppy hat, sighing noisily. Marble's hat was shaped like an oversized tea cosy. (This is because it *was* an over-sized tea cosy – Marble had pinched it from a car-boot sale when she thought no one was watching. She used the spout and handle holes to poke her ears through. It wasn't a good look.) She threw the woolly item carelessly across the room, where it landed, rather unfortunately, on poor

Muffles, who was already more than a little put out at the arrival of Snooks and had been hissing quietly to make a point. A point largely lost on Snooks, who was well used to Muffles's huffiness and was far too friendly a dog to mind what any mere cat thought of him.

It was the discarded tea cosy though that was the last straw for Muffles. She arched her back and bared her teeth and flashed her golden eyes. Sadly this performance only succeeded in making her look more ridiculous, since the outsize cosy was now flopping comically over her small furry face. Pippa bit her top lip hard to stop herself from laughing and gently removed the hat, before leading Snooks over to one of the sweet little dog beds Mrs Fudge had acquired for her customers' pets. Once the terrier was settled snugly on the fluffy bedding with a chewed teddy, a furry yellow frog and a blue-and-white rubber bone, Pippa coaxed Muffles out of the salon and guided her into the kitchen.

She came back just in time to hear Marble utter

 28

the words: 'I need a change, Mrs Fudge, I do. I don't like what you did last time. Not one bit. Quite frankly I am in need of a more *modern* style.' And she thrust her open scrapbook into Mrs Fudge's hands.

Pippa opened her mouth to comment on Marble's rudeness, but Mrs Fudge coughed loudly, peered even more emphatically over the top of her glasses and said carefully, 'I think the kettle has just boiled, Pippa.'

'No, it hasn't,' said Pippa, frowning. 'We've only just—'

'I think it *has*,' said Mrs Fudge. She turned to Marble and fixed a determinedly encouraging smile on her face. 'Now, Marble, let's take a closer look at these styles. I agree it would be lovely to have a New Look for autumn,' she declared. 'Nothing like a New Look to banish those blues.'

Pippa stomped into the kitchen, and Snooks padded out after her in the hope of scavenging some tasty morsels. The pair came back seconds later, Snooks with crumbs all over his mouth and a glint in his eye. Marble was pulling faces at herself in the mirror, twisting her head this way and that.

As if looking at it from a different angle will make it any nicer, Pippa thought grumpily.

She offered Marble some tea in a china cup and saucer with tiny bluebirds painted along the rim. Then she turned her attention to Snooks, who had rolled on to his back in a bid for a marathon-long tummy-tickling session. Pippa happily obliged and soon the pair of them were larking around on the floor, yapping and giggling, a whirl of brown-and-black fur and red stringy plaits.

'I want long blonde flicky luscious locks like *hers*,' Marble announced to Mrs Fudge, suddenly reaching round and stabbing one wrinkled chubby finger at the scrapbook. The teacup teetered in its saucer. Mrs Fudge whisked it to one side before it could spill over the image of a stunningly beautiful actress with long blonde princess-style tresses. She peered at the picture and smiled thinly.

'All right,' she said.

Four hours of bleaching and rinsing, blow-drying and straightening later, Marble did indeed have a hairstyle that resembled, as close as was humanly possible, the image she had stuck into her scrapbook. Unfortunately the hair still framed a face that looked as if it had been run over by a tractor and stamped on with hobnailed boots.

'There!' said Mrs Fudge reassuringly as she showed Marble the back of her head in a hand-held mirror.

Marble grimaced at her reflection. 'Hmm,' she

BEFORE:

AFTER:

said. 'Well, if that's the best you can do, I suppose I'll
have to live with it.'

Pippa was sitting on the counter with Snooks
in her lap. He was now snoring loudly with a very
pleased-with-himself smile on his doggy chops. She
was swinging her long legs and concentrating hard
on *not* saying out loud that she thought that the view
of the back of Marble's head was the best view. She
was bursting with fury at the rudeness of the old
bat. But she knew she wasn't allowed to comment,
so she gave Snooks a vigorous cuddle instead. The

poor pooch awoke with a start. He sneaked a peek at his owner and yelped in surprise. Springing out of Pippa's lap, he went flying through the air and landed on the floor with an ungainly thud. Then he ran to the door, whimpering and quivering while Pippa rushed to his side, speaking soothing words and hiding her smirks in his fur.

'Silly Snooksie!' Mrs Fudge cooed. 'It's only Marble. You know how she likes to change her look now and then.'

Marble was still snarling at her reflection. 'He knows it's me,' she said sneerily. 'He simply doesn't think much of the job you've done. It's a shame you can't do my nails like *hers*,' she added, stabbing at the picture of the film star again. 'Never thought of opening a beauty parlour on the side, I suppose?'

Mrs Fudge took a deep breath and said, 'No, dear. I think I've got my hands full as it is. Talking of which,' she said, making a point of looking at the pocket watch, 'is *that* the time? Pippa dear, will you fetch Marble's hat and coat – and sweep up quickly?

Our next customer will be here shortly.'

Marble heaved herself out of the chair, handed over her payment (and an exceedingly mingy tip), took her tea cosy back from Pippa and crammed it on to her new locks. Mrs Fudge winced as all her hard work was crushed under the woolly monstrosity.

'Come, Snooks. Walkies,' chirruped Marble. The lovely little terrier had perked up at the sight of the ugly old hat and seemed to recognize his owner again. His ears pricked up, he wagged his tail enthusiastically and trotted over to have his lead clipped on to his collar.

Pippa thought wryly that Snooks was a million times easier to please than his crotchety owner, and doubled that thought at Marble's disgruntled words of farewell:

'Let's see if you can do any better next month, Mrs Fudge.'

Mrs Fudge shut the door and shook her head in bewilderment.

'A beauty parlour?' she said. 'Whatever next?'

 34

5

Juicy Gossip at Chop 'n' Chat

Mrs Prim was next. She had come for her 'usual' (blonde highlights) and brought her springer spaniel George with her. George had the silkiest, floppiest ears of any dog Pippa had ever seen, and she enjoyed brushing and stroking them while Mrs Prim sat with her head covered in silver foil and gossiped about boring things such as the weather and the state of the fence in the town park. (Why grown-ups cannot talk about more interesting things, like how clouds can float and why mice like cheese, I do not know, but they don't, so we must just make the best of it.)

'It's just not right,' Mrs Prim wittered, nibbling at the edge of a scone like a nervous hamster. 'The council knows how many dogs there are in the town, and yet they refuse to mend the fence. One of these days my poor Georgie Porgie will go head over heels into the pond. Imagine what that would do to his lovely glossy coat,' she said, pouting and putting on a rather pathetic baby voice.

Muffles, stalking across the top of the counter, let out a voluble purr as if to say, 'Landing in the pond would be too good for that mutt.'

'Muffles!' said Mrs Fudge. 'I hope you're not being rude.'

Pippa looked up from her cross-legged position on the floor where she had been grooming George's fur with one of Mrs Fudge's new hairbrushes. 'Can you understand Muffles, Mrs Fudge?' she asked.

Mrs Prim guffawed with laughter at the very idea. 'How sweet you are!'

Pippa scowled. 'I am *not* sweet.'

DRIING!

'Pippa dear,' said Mrs Fudge hastily, 'that'll be Coral. And don't use my best brushes on the dogs, dear. I've got some old ones out the back

 36

you can have if you really must.'

Coral Jones wanted a perm. She had been wanting a perm for quite some time and Mrs Fudge had been trying for quite some time to advise her against it. ('Her hair's so dry already,' she whispered to Pippa. 'But . . . the customer is always right.')

'A perm it is,' she said to Coral, smiling at her in the mirror.

Coral had brought her pug, Winston. He and George got along very well and were soon chasing each other round and round in circles in the middle of the salon.

'Perhaps you could find the dogs something to do, Pippa dear,' Mrs Fudge said patiently, as Winston

slammed into the back of her legs for the fifth time in a row, knocking the perm lotion flying.

So Pippa found a length of rope which was thick and strong and perfect for chewing on. She put the dogs in a corner and gave them the rope, and they soon got the hang of a lovely game of tug of war, which looked set to keep them occupied – and safely out of the way.

Pippa was now free to see to the customers' refreshments. Making the tea's all very well, but will I ever get my hands on those scissors? she wondered, eyeing them wistfully as she ran back and forth from the kitchen.

Things became even livelier when the Pickle twins, two of the most quarrelsome boys in Crumbly-under-Edge, arrived with their mother.

'Can you give them a bit of a trim?' asked Mrs Pickle breathlessly as she dragged them into the salon kicking and thumping and calling each other the kinds of names that are frankly too stupid to put in a story like this one. 'I'm going to have to dash,

Mrs Fudge. I've just got to do the shopping. I'm sure they'll be as good as gold, won't you, boys?'

Elvis blew a very loud and extremely wet raspberry at Ernie, and Ernie returned the compliment by reaching out and pulling Elvis's right ear so hard Pippa cringed in fear that it might actually come away from the boy's head. At least they don't have a dog, she thought, looking round wildly at the now very cramped salon.

'Now, boys,' said Mrs Fudge, in a commanding tone. Pippa noticed she seemed to have grown several centimetres and was using her over-the-top-of-her-spectacles stare to marvellous effect.

Ernie let go of his brother's ear immediately, and put on a sheepish expression. Elvis stopped yelling and stared at the floor, rubbing his ear sorrowfully. They let themselves be led to the chairs and meekly allowed Pippa to put gowns around them to protect their clothes. Their hair was thick and wavy and seemed to grow in fifty different directions, so cutting it was an afternoon's job in itself, and that was if they managed to sit still.

As Mrs Fudge nipped around the salon from customer to customer, Pippa sat on the counter listening to the gossip, which (although it had not moved on to genuinely fascinating subjects such as what makes snot green or how it was that not everyone could wiggle their ears) was nevertheless perking up a bit.

'I saw Marble's latest look on my way here,' said Mrs Prim pointedly. 'Where on earth did she get the idea for *that* hairstyle?'

'What *does* she look like *this* week?' chipped in Coral.

Mrs Fudge smiled over the top of the twins' heads and said into the mirror, 'Oh, you know Marble. She's always up with the latest fashions.'

Coral rolled her eyes. 'That's not how I would put it,' she said.

Pippa was flicking through magazines. She looked up at this last comment and said, 'Nor would I!'

Mrs Fudge coughed. 'Marble is never satisfied

 40

with her appearance, poor thing. It's a lack of confidence; she needs a lot of jollying along and likes to have a bit of attention.'

Mrs Prim spluttered as she took a sip of tea. 'Likes to be the CENTRE of attention, you mean!' she said.

Coral started giggling.

'Well, we all like to be the centre of attention now and again,' Mrs Fudge said kindly. 'Even the dogs like it, don't you, my dears?' She shot a fond glance at the wrestling pair.

Winston stopped tugging on the rope for an instant and put his head on one side as if to say, 'What are you looking at me like that for?' It was just the break George needed: the spaniel yanked back hard on the rope, freeing it from Winston's jaws. He looked very triumphant for all of a second before he realized he was flying backwards and couldn't stop.

CRASH! The spaniel skidded back into a trolley stacked high with beautifully folded towels, sending

41

the whole lot cascading down in a fluffy rainbow on to the floor.

Pippa sighed and set to work tidying up. The dogs did at least seem rather ashamed of what had happened and retired quietly to a large dog bed where they curled up contentedly together and did not utter another peep.

The only sound now was the vast hairdryer (one of those old-fashioned ones that look as if they would be more at home on an alien spaceship). Coral sat beneath it, her head a dense forest of pink curlers and hairpins. Even the twins were quiet, systematically demolishing a plate of brownies, so Pippa swung herself up on to the countertop and sucked contentedly on a fizzy raspberry lollipop.

Minutes later the doorbell rang again and Pippa ran to answer it. As she opened the door, it let in a blast of icy air and a whirlwind of golden-brown leaves. A tall dark man glided through as if carried along by the flurry. He had long black hair, braided and hanging in snaky strips, and a smile as white and gleaming as a string of pearls. I say he 'glided in', not because he was especially elegant but because he really actually *did* glide rather than walk.

He was on Rollerblades, you see.

'Hello, darlin'! Post's up!' He grinned at Pippa and winked. 'I'll take it through. Morning, darlin's!' he shouted to the salon at large.

'Hello, Raphael,' the ladies chorused. Coral, out from under the dryer, gave a flutter of her eyelashes for good measure, Pippa noticed.

Over in the corner George let forth a lusty bark and Winston stiffly extricated himself from the dog basket, giving himself a quick shake. Both dogs trotted over to say hello. Raphael threw them each a biscuit from the stash deep in his pockets.

Then he took a step back and wobbled slightly on his Rollerblades. 'Man!' he breathed, clutching on to the side of the counter for support. 'If that isn't the holiest vision I ever did see. Mrs Fudge, who is this bee-oo-tiful ladeee?' he crooned.

43

Coral burst into an uncontrollable torrent of
high-pitched giggles and flapped a hand modestly.
'Oh, really, Raphael. Don't!' she tittered.

Pippa's eyebrows knitted together in puzzlement.
'That lady is obviously Coral!' she exclaimed. 'Is
something wrong with your eyes, Raphael? Maybe
you should get some glasses. If you can't see too
well, maybe Mrs Fudge could lend you hers. Or
maybe—'

Raphael let rip with a belly-buster of a laugh.

 44

'Ooooh! You are a sweetheart, Miss Pippa!' he guffawed.

He flicked quickly through a bundle of letters, glancing at the addresses on the envelopes, and niftily pulled out a few for Mrs Fudge. Then, throwing them in the air in an arc, he whistled as they landed in a neat pile on the countertop.

'Mmm,' he said dreamily, sniffing the air. 'It's cupcakes today, no? Or is that an aroma of chocolate brownies I is detectin' there?'

'There *are* some brownies as it happens. Would you like one?' Pippa asked.

Raphael winked. 'Two cakes would be even better,' he said cheekily, touching his hat like an old-fashioned gentleman.

Pippa nodded and zipped into the kitchen. She returned with one brownie, one scone and a cup of tea.

Raphael licked his lips dramatically and took them from her. 'Thank you, sweetness!' he sang. 'Let me tell you, you'll think I'm *wort'* two cakes when you hear the news I got,' he said mysteriously.

'That sounds interesting,' said Mrs Fudge, putting down her comb and turning to face him properly.

Mrs Prim stopped flicking the pages of her magazine. Coral stopped trying to see the back of her head in the mirror. Even the twins momentarily looked up from punching one another.

'There's a new kid in town,' whispered Raphael dramatically.

'A new *kid*?' Pippa repeated. 'What do you mean? A girl like me? A boy? A baby goat?'

'No, sweetness. I mean a new person – a newcomer.' He looked at Mrs Fudge. 'You know that rickety-pickety building by the town hall?'

'The old coffee shop?' she said.

'That' the one – all boarded up and with dem scruffy, mucky posters stuck on the walls and the brickwork tumblin' down,' said Raphael, grimacing.

Everyone in the salon nodded and murmured, pulling similar faces of dislike and disapproval. The building Raphael was talking about was an

 46

embarrassing eyesore in Crumbly-under-Edge. The townspeople had been saying for a couple of years that it should be demolished if no one was going to use it, but still it stood there, like a blackened rotten tooth in a line of shiny healthy ones.

'Well,' said Raphael, leaning forward. He looked especially mischievous and naughty. 'Somebody movin' in!' He whispered the words hoarsely, his eyes wide.

Mrs Prim gasped.

Coral Jones squealed.

George yelped and Winston snored.

The twins yawned and went back to giving one another dead arms.

Pippa shrugged and said what the twins (and no doubt you, dear reader) were thinking: 'What is so exciting about someone moving into a tumbledown pile of old bricks, for goodness sake?'

Mrs Fudge smiled and said, 'Think about it. No one moves anywhere round here, dear.'

Raphael laughed and nodded in agreement. 'Too

true! Nobody has moved to Crumbly-under-Edge for years and *years*, darlin'.'

Mrs Fudge's timer, which she used to remind her when to wash out people's hair dye and highlights, chose this moment to ring very shrilly, which was a bit of a shock for all concerned as they had been concentrating so hard on what Raphael had been saying. Everyone jumped, including poor Winston, who had been in the middle of a particularly delicious dream featuring sausages.

Elvis made good use of the distraction to twist his brother's arm even harder.

'Yowch!' shrieked Ernie.

'And would you happen to know who this newcomer is?' Mrs Fudge shouted above the chaos and commotion.

'Not yet, but I will soon, o' course! I'm the postie. I know every*ting* and every*one* in this town,' he said, waving a long finger at Mrs Fudge in mock remonstration. 'Something tellin' me there could be a shakin' up o' tings around here.' He winked and

 48

nodded knowingly. 'You don't have a mystery new arrival like this without some big changes – you'll see.'

Then, draining his tea in one noisy slurp, he popped the entire brownie into his mouth and wedged the scone on to the top of his hat for later.

'Right, I's away now!' he called, pushing back from the countertop and rollerblading out of the salon. He waved goodbye with one long, lanky arm. 'Don't you worry, Mrs F. I'll keep you posted – cos that's what I do, darlin'!'

6

The Queen of America – Or Is It?

Everyone in Crumbly-under-Edge could think of little else but the old coffee shop.

'It would be nice if it was a coffee shop again.'

'Oh no. I don't like coffee. How about a sandwich shop?'

'I saw the painters and decorators there the other day.'

'I saw a delivery van turn up.'

'I bet it'll be turned into flats.'

'I think it's going to rain.'

'Could be a cheese shop. What do you think of cheese?'

I hope you keel over from boredom from your own boring conversations, Pippa thought irritably as she skateboarded past the gossiping Crumblies on her way to Chop 'n' Chat one Saturday.

She generally found that whizzing about on her skateboard was the best way to catch secret snippets of conversation, as she moved so fast people didn't break off to say hello; they just kept on gossiping. Sadly the snippets of gossip had all been about the same thing for the past few weeks, and as dull as could be, as far as Pippa was concerned.

She propped her skateboard up in the porch and let herself in with the key Mrs Fudge had entrusted her with. She kicked off her shoes and hung her red duffel coat on the peg.

'Hello, Mrs Fudge! It's mee-eee!' she called as she skipped down the hall.

Mrs Fudge emerged from the kitchen, wearing her blue-and-white daisy apron and washing-up gloves to match. Her rosy cheeks glowed at the sight of her favourite little helper. 'Just in time for a cup of something, dear,' she cooed, handing her a chipped mug of sweet-smelling hot chocolate.

'Now, what do you think about this? I had a call yesterday from a *new* customer.'

Pippa blew on her drink to cool it and raised her eyebrows to show she was listening. (Not that I am suggesting for one minute that she was listening with her eyebrows, but she couldn't talk because she was blowing, so she had to use her eyebrows as a means of communication instead.)

'Yes, a lady called Trinity Meddler phoned and asked if she could have an appointment today.'

Pippa slurped her drink and said, 'Mmmm!' She knew she should ask more questions, as this woman was clearly the person everyone in Crumbly-under-Edge had been waiting for, but she was frankly a bit fed up with all the gossip by now and couldn't have cared less if the new person had been the Queen of America.

'It's really quite exciting!' Mrs Fudge was saying. 'I haven't had a *new* customer for years and years. Your job, dear, will be to take her coat and make her a cup of tea and so on. But I don't want you to be too nosy and ask her lots of questions.'

Pippa frowned. 'I am never nosy and I never ask lots of questions,' she objected. 'I only chatter politely to people, like you do.'

Mrs Fudge smiled and said gently, 'All I'm saying is we don't know this lady, do we? So we must be on our best behaviour and make her feel welcome.'

'Yes, Mrs Fudge,' said Pippa, blowing on her drink again.

She looked out of the window. For the first time in quite a long while the weather had decided to put its best foot forward. The leaves shone golden and red and bronze in the sun's rays, and the grass shimmered dazzlingly with spots of diamond-bright dew. The sky was like a clean sheet of blue paper, with no messy clouds or even the slightest hint of a scribble from an aeroplane's engines, and the birds sounded as though they were putting in some early practice for their spring performance, they were singing so loudly.

Pippa sighed. Nothing bad could possibly happen on a day like this.

DRIIIIIIIINNNNNNGG!!

'Goodness!' exclaimed Mrs Fudge, jumping at the sound of the doorbell. Her hot chocolate jumped too and some of it landed on the front of her apron. 'Oh dear me. Pippa, would you—?'

DRIIIIIIIIIIINNNNNNNNNGGGGG!

Pippa slammed her mug down on the counter and ran into the hall with Mrs Fudge trotting along behind her, puffing and panting as she hurried to remove her apron and tidy herself. She glanced at the grandfather clock in the hall. 'It can't be the new customer. It's not even nine—!'

DRIIIIIIIIIIINNNNNNNNNNNNGGGGGGGGG!

 54

Pippa flung open the door just as the visitor's finger leaped back from the doorbell. The stranger was standing so close to the door that Pippa toppled backwards and fell into poor Mrs Fudge, who was right behind her.

'Oh, I'm terribly sorry,' said the woman, with a sugary-sweet smile. 'I didn't mean to *alarm* you. I thought the bell wasn't working – couldn't hear it from out here,' she added, tilting her head demurely.

Pippa narrowed her eyes and gave the stranger an appraising look. Either the woman was deaf or she was lying. Raphael had bought Mrs Fudge a new front doorbell after Marble had complained about the old one, and he had installed it and tested it personally. It was the loudest money could buy, on account of the fact that many of Mrs Fudge's clients were not exactly blessed in the hearing department.

'So, may I come in?' the woman asked, a hint of sourness now creeping into her voice.

'Er, yes,' Pippa mumbled, moving aside.

The woman tossed her head haughtily and

stepped gracefully into the hall. Pippa looked her up and down: she was as tall and spindly as Mrs Fudge was short and cuddly, and decidedly sharper and spikier-looking than the old lady. Her hair was as glossy and smooth and inkily black as Mrs Fudge's was fluffy and curly and snowily white, and it was cut so neatly along her jawline it looked as though you might slice your fingers on it if you touched it. (It certainly did *not* look in need of Mrs Fudge's attention.) Her face was chiselled, with cheeks that looked permanently sucked-in and lips that were ever so slightly too big. Her nose was long and pointy and just a tiny bit beaky, and her eyebrows were so thin and dark Pippa wondered if they were drawn on with a pencil. Alarmingly spidery eyelashes framed eyes that flashed like steel. Pippa found she could not look at them for long without feeling decidedly uncomfortable.

As the newcomer crossed the threshold a strong perfume filled the air. It was a strange, heady scent, but Pippa was distracted from trying to work out exactly what the aroma was by something soft brushing against her legs. 'Oh!' she cried, glancing down. 'You've got a dog!'

Quite an adorable little dog, in fact. A poodle as cottonwool white as its owner's hair was ebony black. It was very quiet too, which is why Pippa had only noticed it as it swept past her leg.

'What a *cute* dog!' she cooed, bending down to pat its head. It was wearing a diamanté collar with a tag saying 'Gorgeous'. Bit showy-offy, Pippa thought. But still cute.

The poodle fixed her with a cool stare. Then, so only Pippa could hear, it let out a very low growl. Pippa straightened up immediately and said quaveringly, 'Er, yes, anyway, come in.' She pressed herself against the wall, keeping one wary eye on the dog.

Mrs Fudge bustled forward with a huge fussy welcome, making sure Pippa took the woman's coat.

Honestly, thought Pippa, anyone would think she really *was* the Queen of America.

She followed the two women into the salon. They were already deep in conversation, Mrs Fudge's voice chitter-chattering away in its light, birdlike tones and the stranger's voice answering, smooth and silky as chocolate. And all the while the poodle was watching Pippa, its eyes narrowed, its lips pulled back just enough to show alarmingly sharp, fine white teeth. She was glad that the animal couldn't talk. It probably would not have had anything friendly to say. Quite suddenly, as though reading her thoughts, it let out a harsh, 'Yap, yap, yappity-yap!'

Pippa shuddered.

At last Mrs Fudge turned to her, beaming, and said, 'Let me introduce you. This is Ms Trinity

Meddler; Trinity, meet my wonderful assistant, Pippa Peppercorn.'

Trinity looked Pippa up and down as if she were something on a shelf in a shop. 'Your *assistant*, you say?'

This was said with such syrupy sweetness that Pippa felt sure there was a meaning behind these words that she couldn't quite grasp. She felt confused and cross at the same time and could only answer, 'Hmmm,' and glare at this person who was stooping to take a closer look at her, as though she had been relegated to the 'bargain basement' shelf due to a defect in her appearance.

Mrs Fudge twittered, 'Well, yes. I know she's young, but she's a complete dear. Wouldn't know what to do without her! Pippa, make us some tea and fetch some of those almond biscuits I made yesterday, can you? Oh, and what about your darling little dog? What would she like?'

'Foo-Foo? Oh, *he's* quite a fussy eater. He won't have anything, thank you.'

'Foo-Foo?' Pippa repeated, with a splutter of incredulous laughter. '*He*?'

'Yes,' said Trinity coldly, one eyebrow raised in challenge.

An awkward silence descended and began spreading its tentacles into the room.

'An adorable name for an adorable pooch,' said Mrs Fudge firmly. 'Off you go now, Pippa.'

'Yap, yappity-yap!' chimed Foo-Foo as if agreeing with Mrs Fudge.

Pippa sloped off to the kitchen muttering, 'Whoever heard of putting a diamanté collar with the word "gorgeous" on a *boy* dog?'

She returned to find Foo-Foo curled up on the sofa near the till, which was Muffles's favourite place.

Unfortunately Muffles chose that moment to trot into the salon, nose held high, toes ballerina-light on the lino floor. She was making her way towards the sofa when she stopped, one paw in mid-air. She sniffed delicately. Gradually the scents she picked up triggered a warning in her feline brain and she

 60

carefully put her paw down, lowered her head and scanned the room, eyes narrowed. That was when she saw Foo-Foo, whose ears were pointing to attention and whose mouth had turned distinctly snarly.

'YOOOOOOOWWWWWWUUUUULLL!' screeched Muffles, rocketing into the air in a ball of spiky rage, her sharp teeth bared, her eyes bulging as though someone had just stuck a red-hot poker in her face.

'Poor Muffles!' Pippa cried, flying to the cat's side and bundling her into her arms with lots of crooning 'There-there's and 'Poor puss-cat's.

'Is your cat normally like that?' Trinity asked, cautiously leaning back in her chair as if to shield herself from attack.

'Oh, she can be a bit territorial at times,' Mrs Fudge said dismissively.

'I don't blame her! It's because that ridiculous poodle is sitting in her place!' Pippa exclaimed.

Mrs Fudge made a flapping gesture with her free hand and said, 'Honestly, Pippa. It's not Muffles's place! It's only a sofa. She doesn't own it.'

'Yap, yappity-yap!' said Foo-Foo smugly.

I could shoot that animal, thought Pippa.

Trinity looked up from a pile of magazines she had been sifting through (as though they were particularly smelly bits of rubbish) and said, 'Oh my dear Mrs Fudge, what sweet *old-fashioned* publications you have here. You don't have anything a little more . . . up to date? I was hoping for a modern twist on my trusty bob. Something to wow the townsfolk with when I open my *new business*. Never mind, I shall simply opt for a wash and blow-dry, thank you.'

At the words 'new business', Muffles struggled out of Pippa's arms. Her ears were flattened and her back arched in furry feline fury.

'Muffles – *dear*!' admonished Mrs Fudge. 'Anyone would think she had never seen a dog before! What was that you were saying about a new business, Trinity?'

The newcomer proceeded to tell Mrs Fudge in some detail about her purchase of the old coffee shop.

'Such a *darling* little place. I mean, it will be when *I've* finished with it,' Trinity gushed. 'Obviously at the moment it's a *wreck*. But it's just the perfect location for my beauty salon.'

'Beauty salon?' Pippa parroted.

'Yes. "Heaven on Earth" I shall call it. Perhaps you could be my first customer, Mrs Fudge.'

Mrs Fudge flushed and mumbled about having no use for beauty salons at her age.

'Nonsense!' cried Trinity. 'We businesswomen must stick together. We can pass customers on to each other—'

'It's all right.' Pippa couldn't help butting in. 'We've already got loads of customers, thanks.'

Trinity narrowed her eyes and said, 'I'm sure you do. Well, how about this: I shall come to you for my hair, and you, Mrs Fudge, shall come to me for little pampering sessions? Hard-working ladies deserve to treat themselves now and again.'

'What about me?' Pippa butted in again, somewhat resentfully this time. 'I am a hard-working lady too!'

Trinity let a tinkly laugh trip out of her perfectly painted purple lips and said, 'Oh, sweet! I think you'll have to ask your mummy if she'll let you come. Most of my treatments are for grown-ups only,' she added, leaning out from the chair to pat Pippa on the arm.

 64

Pippa jerked her arm back as though she had been stung. She had by now decided she most definitely did not like Trinity Meddler, and if it hadn't been for the very clear do-not-say-a-word signals that Mrs Fudge was sending her from over the top of her spectacles, she would have said as much there and then.

She was considering whether or not to start sulking when the doorbell rang.

'Go and answer that, will you, Pippa?' Mrs Fudge asked as she covered Trinity Meddler in a pink-and-orange overall and patted a red towel down over her shoulders.

Pippa rolled her eyes rudely and dragged her feet out into the hallway.

If her heart had been heavy before, the silhouette behind the dappled glass in the door did nothing to lighten it.

It was Marble Wainwright.

7

Marble Goes Loopy

Pippa opened the door and muttered, 'Morning,' as Marble stumbled in, clutching at her headscarf with one hand and Snooks's lead with the other. Her dowdy grey overcoat billowed in the strong gust of wind that blew in the door behind her, giving her the appearance of a dirty old ship in full sail.

Gosh, Pippa thought, glancing at the sky, which was as dark as mud and twice as dirty. What's happened to the blue skies and sunshine?

'Here,' Marble grunted. She wrenched her overcoat off in an ungainly manner and threw it at poor Pippa, who stumbled backwards under its weight. 'She ready for me?' Marble said, nodding in the direction of the salon with her characteristic lack of grace. She removed her headscarf to reveal a bedraggled mop of stringy yellow hair. The phrase 'dragged through a haystack backwards' sprang to Pippa's mind. It was bewildering how quickly and thoroughly Marble had managed to undo Mrs Fudge's hard work.

Snooks was straining at his leash and jumped up, panting eagerly, so Pippa bent down to pat him before bothering to answer Marble. Then she carelessly flung the coat and scarf on a peg and said sharply, 'No, actually. She's got a new customer with her.'

At this Marble's puddingy face lit up and a grimace split her features in two (which, Pippa knew, was the closest Marble ever managed to come to smiling). 'Ah, a *new* customer, is it?' she said, showing none-too-shiny teeth. 'It'll be someone to do with that coffee shop. Let's see then.' She pushed past Pippa, giving her a sharp jab with her elbow for good measure, and waddled her way into the salon.

'Cooeee!' she called in a fakely posh voice. 'Mrs

67

Fuu-uudge, your favourite customer is here!'

Pippa came in behind her, holding on to Snooks's lead and pulling a face as though she was being sick.

Mrs Fudge was busy running her hands over Trinity's sleek black bob and saying things like, 'What wonderful thick hair you have, Ms Meddler,' and 'I must say it will be a pleasure to work with hair that's been so beautifully cared for.'

Marble coughed loudly. Mrs Fudge looked up and said politely, 'I'll be with you in a minute, Marble. And how are you today?'

But unfortunately, before Marble could answer, the calm in the salon was ruined by Foo-Foo. He had been sitting very contentedly on Muffles's sofa, but one look at Snooks and the funny little poodle went berserk. He leaped in the air, legs splayed, as though someone had swapped the sofa for a bed of nails. His tongue shot out, his ears went back and he let forth an avalanche of high-pitched barking.

'Yap, yap, yappity-yap! Yap, yap, yappity-yap! Yap, yap, yappity-yap!'

Snooks pulled so savagely at his lead that he wrenched himself free of Pippa's grasp, sending her flying backwards. He barked with glee, as if a particularly raucous game of chase had just been announced, and went tearing after the poodle, sending the twirly-whirly chairs spinning like tops.

Trinity had turned bright red in the face and, oddly, appeared to have tears in her eyes. Marble started shrieking, and Pippa herself was trying not to cry because she had scraped her elbow.

'Enough!' cried Mrs Fudge.

Snooks skidded to a halt mid-chase. Even Foo-Foo stopped barking and stared at Mrs Fudge in outraged disbelief. (He was not a dog who was accustomed to being ordered about.)

'Pippa dear, go into the kitchen and get yourself a plaster for your elbow from the first-aid kit. I'll be with you in a minute. And take Snooks with you. I cannot work in such chaos.'

'Yes, Mrs Fudge.' Pippa took hold of the scruffy terrier by the collar, glad to be allowed to get away from her least favourite person (Marble) and her new-also-least-favourite person (Trinity). She had reached the door to the kitchen when she heard a loud sniffing noise and turned to see Trinity, tears now streaming down her face, dabbing at her cheeks with a handkerchief.

'My dear Ms Meddler, I am so sorry,' Mrs Fudge said, her face creased with worry. 'Are you feeling all right?'

'It is I who am sorry, Mrs Fudge,' said Trinity in a small voice, pressing the hanky into her eyes and sniffing loudly. 'I should leave immediately. I . . . The whole thing's just too upsetting for words.'

'No, no! It's quite all right,' said Mrs Fudge anxiously. 'These things happen with dogs sometimes, don't they? We are quite used to it here.'

Pippa gulped, feeling more than a bit embarrassed at seeing a grown woman sobbing over a mere dog scuffle. She shot a swift glance across at Marble, expecting her to make some sarcastic comment. But Marble was staring at the scene open-mouthed and,

 70

it seemed, for once at a complete loss for words.

Mrs Fudge peered at her over the top of her glasses. 'Are *you* all right, Marble?' she was asking, concerned and puzzled by the calamitous turn of events. 'You've gone quite white. Dearie, dearie me. What a morning! Pippa! Run and fetch Marble a glass of water.'

Pippa peered in wonder. Marble did look ghostly pale. Although her lips moved, no sound came from her mouth. Pippa did run and fetch her a glass of water then, and pressing it into Marble's shaking hands she guided her to a chair. Mrs Fudge bustled around her, loosening her cardigan and fanning her face with a magazine. Soon the translucent look of nausea had left Marble's features and was replaced by a strange dreamy gaze at Trinity. Pippa realized that Trinity was staring coolly back, her head held high, a tiny triumphant smile playing in the corners of her mouth. She seemed to have recovered remarkably quickly from her tearfulness.

Marble raised a shaky hand and pointed one chubby finger at Trinity.

71

She looks like a zombie, Pippa thought.

'I – I want to look like that,' Marble said in a whisper.

'Sorry, dear?' said Mrs Fudge, shooting Pippa a concerned glance.

'All my life,' Marble said huskily, 'I have been searching for the perfect look. I have scoured newspapers and magazines for pictures and I have been coming to you for advice, Mrs Fudge. But this – this vision of perfection before me . . . !' Her voice petered out in a croak and she clutched her wrinkly hands to her chest. 'You have to make me look like *her*!'

There followed a silence that could have sunk a thousand ships (if, that is, it had suddenly turned into a vastly huge and massively heavy thing that someone had dropped from a ginormous height).

Pippa felt extremely uncomfortable. It was as if she and Mrs Fudge had walked in on a very personal and private scene of a yucky and soppy romantic nature.

Marble eventually broke the silence with five simple words: '*Never — seen — anyone — so — beautiful!*'

Clearing her throat, Trinity said, 'Mrs Fudge, aren't you going to introduce me to your charming friend?'

Mrs Fudge said, 'Of course,' in a dreamy, hypnotic tone. 'Marble, this is Trinity. Trinity — Marble.'

Then, giving herself a shake, she gestured to Pippa to follow her into the kitchen, leaving Marble chattering with Trinity about the benefits of extending, removing and improving all manner of baffling bodily things.

Snooks greeted Pippa and Mrs Fudge with much jumping and yapping, presumably comforted at the thought that he was not going to be shut away in the kitchen forever and forgotten about. (Dogs can be daft like that.)

Pippa caught him in her arms as he bounded up and proceeded to wash her face with lots of tickly licks of joy. She giggled and put him down. 'That's enough of that, Snooks,' she said. 'Mrs Fudge wants to talk to me.'

'I do indeed, dear,' said Mrs Fudge emphatically. 'What on *earth* do you make of Marble?' she asked, as she put the kettle on.

Pippa snorted and folded her arms crossly. 'What I make of it is that Marble is never nice to *us*, but she is being distinctly slimy and greasy in her niceness to that new person – who was also acting pretty strangely. I don't think she was really crying just then, you know.'

But Mrs Fudge wasn't listening; she was tapping her fingers distractedly on the kitchen table. 'I

 74

do hope Marble hasn't gone and got her hopes up again,' she said sorrowfully. 'I will do my best with her hair, but I can't very well make a short, er, rounded middle-aged lady look like a tall, slim younger lady, now can I?'

The kettle let forth a high-pitched whistle which brought Mrs Fudge back to the present. She busied herself with making a fresh pot of tea in her favourite bone-china teapot decorated with ducks and chickens and seemed to have momentarily forgotten about Marble.

Pippa, however, was boiling with fury that the arrival of this new person could throw everyone into such a frenzy. Who did she think she was? And as for her ridiculous poodle . . .

Mrs Fudge held the tea tray out to Pippa so she had to uncross her arms to take it.

'Come and have a nice cup of tea with us,' she coaxed. 'We mustn't abandon our customers.'

As they went back into the salon it seemed, however, that the customers weren't bothered about being abandoned. Quite the contrary: in fact Marble and Trinity had their heads together in a very conspiratorial manner.

As Mrs Fudge and Pippa entered, they were just in time to hear Trinity say to Marble, 'I'm sure we can discuss a special discount for *you*, my dear.'

8

A Little Bit of Heaven on Earth

There's something strange in the air, thought Pippa as she made her way to Chop 'n' Chat the next week.

It's true that there had been a dramatic change in the weather: the brief spell of sunshine had completely disappeared and the blue skies had flown south for the winter.

Maybe it's not the weather, but whatever it is, it's making my hair go all crackly. I can just feel that things are topsy-turvy and plain *wrong*.

She entered the salon to find Coral Jones was already there. Her perm had gone flat in the rain and she'd come to have highlights instead – at least, that was what she said. The truth was, after Raphael, Coral was possibly the most eager gossipmonger in Crumbly-under-Edge. And when she had news to share, there was no stopping her.

'She pops by once in a while to check on the building work apparently. I hear she's *incredibly* glamorous,' babbled Coral, in a knowing tone. She was talking to Mrs Fudge's reflection while the kindly hairdresser divided her hair into sections to touch up the dark roots which were showing through (a nightmare for ladies like Coral, let me tell you, who don't want anyone to know their true hair colour).

'Yes,' said Mrs Fudge simply. 'Ms Meddler certainly turns heads.'

'You've *met* her?' Coral breathed, turning to face Mrs Fudge.

'Oh, we've *met* her,' Pippa said with heavy sarcasm. Mrs Fudge winked at her while Coral rattled on.

 78

'I hear she's opening a new business. Nice that the coffee shop will be used properly and not just converted into flats, isn't it?' she tittered.

It was obvious to Pippa what Coral was doing: sniffing around for more information. Just like her pug, Winston, sniffing around the floor for crumbs.

'Yes, a beauty business,' said Mrs Fudge. She concentrated on folding the sections of Coral's hair into strips of tin foil slowly and deliberately. Pippa glanced at her dear friend: the little old lady, who was usually so jolly and rosy-cheeked, today looked worn down; her face was tinged with grey and her snow-white hair had lost some of its bounce.

She's worried, Pippa thought.

'Well, it's rather nice to have a beauty salon in Crumbly-under-Edge,' replied Coral. 'Perhaps we'll all be a little less crumbly around the edges from now on!' And she giggled, pleased with her silly joke.

Pippa bristled. 'You've got Mrs Fudge to make you all look smart and lovely,' she snapped. 'Isn't that enough?'

79

Coral stammered, 'I – I – yes, of course. I didn't mean . . .'

But she was saved from saying what she had meant by the arrival of Raphael.

'Helllooooo, darlin's!' he cried as he zoomed into the salon. 'I has a *stack* of excitin'-lookin' post for y'all today! And I saw Coral comin' along here this mornin' so I thought I'd bring hers here too. You don't mind, do you now, Coral my sweetness?'

Coral's blush deepened, making her look even dafter than she already did with her head full of tin foil.

Mrs Fudge stopped painting Coral's head with the dye and gave Raphael a watery smile. 'How lovely of you, Raphael dear. Pippa – teatime!'

Pippa had never been happier to see the friendly postman. She scuttled out to make tea as Raphael's booming voice filled the salon with cheery chatter. But her heart sank as she heard him say, 'So, what is we all tinkin' about this Heaven on Earth place, den?'

Have people really got nothing better to talk about than that nasty woman and her stupid beauty parlour? Pippa thought angrily. She turned the tap on too hard and the water gushed out with such force that most of it rebounded into her face.

'Baaahflflfllgle!' she spluttered, groping blindly for the tap to turn it off.

She re-emerged into the salon a few minutes later, having tried to dry herself with a tea towel but knowing that she still probably resembled a drowned rat.

Mrs Fudge looked at Pippa quizzically as she came in and set down a tray of tea things. 'Oh dear,' she said. 'I think we need to tidy you up. Just let me finish with Coral and set the timer.'

Raphael was biting his lips, quite clearly trying not to laugh.

'I don't know why you are all so happy!' Pippa blurted out. 'I've met this new person and she is utterly slimy and horrible and her dog is—'

'*Pippa*,' said Mrs Fudge warningly.

But both of them were interrupted by a loud squeal from Coral, who was reading one of the letters Raphael had given her.

'She's having a party! And she's invited *me*!' she exclaimed, a hand flying to her face. 'Oh my goodness. Oh dear, oh dear. Mrs Fudge, do you think these highlights will be all right for a glamorous party?'

'What is you filly-fallyin' about?' Raphael asked. 'Who is havin' a glam-or-ous party? I hope they is invitin' me!'

Coral waved a delicate piece of cream paper edged with gold, and stabbed at it with a finger. A waft of heavy perfume filled the air. Pippa wrinkled her nose in distaste and craned her neck to take a look at the wording of the invitation.

Come and find a little bit of

✦☆ **HEAVEN ON EARTH** ☆✦

Trinity Meddler invites you to spend an evening celebrating the opening of her new beauty salon

On *Friday 21 September at 8 p.m.*

Champagne and nibbles
Dress: Heavenly!

Pippa made a gesture which quite plainly said, 'I'm going to be sick.'

'It's from *her*,' Coral said, her voice hushed with awe. 'Trinity Meddler has sent me a personal invitation to her opening night.'

Mrs Fudge looked at the invitation and said casually, 'Pippa dear, have you looked through my post yet?'

'I'm just looking now,' Pippa replied, ripping open bills and catalogues and all the boring post that seems to stream through people's letter boxes these days, even in Crumbly-under-Edge. 'I, er, Raphael, is there a gold-edged envelope you might have missed?'

Raphael looked awkward and made a show of rummaging deep in his post bag. 'I must admit, sweetness, there is no envelope that I have missed. But I might have made a mistake in the post office, darlin',' he added hastily.

Everyone knew, however, that Raphael never made mistakes with the post.

'I'll go back at the end of me rounds and have a good check,' he assured them. 'I'm sure you'll not have been missed out, Mrs F. I'll keep you posted!' he cried, pushing off from the counter and rollerblading his way out into the hall.

'Raphael, your tea!' Mrs Fudge called out after him.

But the postie had gone.

9

Panicky Party Preparations

It appeared that Mrs Fudge did not have an invitation to the party. Raphael came back later that day to deliver the news, but by that time Mrs Fudge had prepared herself for disappointment.

'Always look on the bright side, Pippa my dear,' she said calmly, once she had listened to Pippa rant and rave for the millionth time about how she didn't like the look of Trinity Meddler *or* her poodle and that frankly not being invited to the party was the very last straw, even if it was a stupid party for stupid people that she wouldn't go to if you paid her.

'And the bright side is what exactly?' Pippa huffed, swinging her legs violently against the counter.

'Don't do that, dear, you'll chip the paint,' Mrs Fudge remonstrated. 'The bright side of this situation is that, if there's going to be a party, lots of people will want to have their hair done.'

Pippa scowled. 'Why are you being so cheery, Mrs Fudge?'

'Because I cannot see any reason not to be. Smile and the world smiles with you, cry and you cry alone!' she trilled, picking up the phone as it started to ring.

'Hello, Chop 'n' Chat, Mrs Fudge speaking!' she sang. 'Ah, Mrs Juniper. Yes, of course I can fit you in, dear . . .'

The phone rang and rang all morning, until Pippa was sure it would explode from such constant use. Mrs Fudge was right – the party *did* mean good business: she was fully booked all week. Every single day from nine o'clock in the morning until six o'clock at night customers streamed through Chop 'n' Chat, bringing their chatter and their dogs with them. Mrs Fudge asked Pippa to work after school as well, and Pippa was glad to help.

'They're in a right old tizz about this party, aren't they?' said Mrs Fudge as she instructed Pippa on how to mix up a particularly lurid hair dye for a lady who wanted her hair piled on top of her head in a pink ice-cream-like confection.

'They've all gone stark raving loony,' muttered Pippa.

I have to say (if I was to be asked) I agree with Pippa. Penelope Smythe wanted green-and-purple streaks with her hair brushed every which way. ('She looks like a multicoloured porcupine,' hissed Pippa.) Millicent Beadle wanted yellow-and-black streaks and insisted on her hair being cut very short and then made spiky with enough hair gel to glue a jumbo jet's wings on. ('Looks like a big fat furry bumble bee to me,' Pippa scoffed.) And Mary Stott, normally the quietest and mousiest of Chop 'n' Chat's regulars, sheepishly explained that she wanted, 'Long red hair set in corkscrew curls like a mermaid's.' Even Pippa was lost for words at that.

87

Penelope Smythe

Millicent Beadle

Ma[r]
Sto[r]

Friday, the day of the party itself, was the busiest day. Luckily that Friday had been announced as a school holiday. (The teachers had said they needed the day off to plan lessons and discuss Forward Thinking and Educational Philosophy, but everyone knew that they were actually getting ready for the party too.) Pippa was on the one hand utterly fed up and disgusted at the Crumblies' complete obsession with Trinity Meddler's party, and on the other completely thrilled at the prospect of a day off school.

'Can you be here at seven o'clock on Friday morning, dear?' Mrs Fudge asked. The old lady looked so crumpled and worried, raking her small hands through her fluffy white hair and frowning over the top of her half-moon spectacles, that Pippa felt her heart do a backflip followed by a bellyflop. She flung her arms around Mrs Fudge and hugged her tight, saying, 'I'll be here at six if you want me to.'

The old lady smiled and patted her head. 'Seven will do just nicely. We can have a spot of breakfast together, get the salon ready and plan the day.'

That day certainly was the busiest Pippa had ever known. She flew in and out of the kitchen with plates and trays overflowing with goodies, while Mrs Fudge snipped and washed and set and primped and curled and dyed and dried and gelled and moussed and set and sprayed. And all the while the air was humming with chatter and natter, and the floor was covered with snoozing and snuffling dogs. Even *they* seemed to find the end-of-week atmosphere quite exhausting.

Coral was one of the last customers. 'I'm all

a-flutter!' she trilled, as she sat down and beamed at her reflection. 'Mrs Fudge, what on earth can you do with my hair to make me look gorgeous enough for the party tonight?'

Winston chose that moment to bark very loudly indeed.

Pippa thought that if he could talk he would probably be saying, 'You can't do anything, Mrs Fudge. Coral will never look gorgeous.'

And if you think that's mean, you have to understand that Pippa was still feeling very prickly about the fact that she and Mrs Fudge were the only two people who had not been asked to the opening night of Heaven on Earth.

'I think we should go anyway,' Pippa had said while they were eating their breakfast that morning.

'No, dear. That's called gatecrashing, and I have no intention of being a gatecrasher,' Mrs Fudge had said firmly.

'But what if there isn't a gate in front of Heaven on Earth?' Pippa had protested loudly.

'It doesn't matter,' Mrs Fudge had said with a wry smile. 'Gate or no gate, I am not attending a party to which I have not been invited.'

In actual fact no one knew whether or not there *was* a gate in front of the new beauty salon. This was because the whole time it was being refurbished there were huge wooden hoardings up in front of it to hide the work that was being done. The grand unveiling was to happen on the night of the party.

'I am sure it'll be simply *glitzy* after everything I've heard about her,' gabbled Coral. 'Marble says it's bound to be classy and tasteful. Marble says she's the most sophisticated person she has ever met.'

'*Marble* says,' Pippa parroted in a sing-songy voice (under her breath).

Mrs Fudge flicked her a warning look over her glasses and then said, 'I am sure we can make you look just the part, Coral dear. How about a nice wash with my new range of Luscious Strawberry shampoo and conditioner? Pippa, you can wash Coral's hair today. And then we'll give you a lovely blow-dry. I don't think your colour needs any touching up.'

Coral pulled a face at her reflection. 'I was hoping for something more special. I don't want to walk out of here looking *ordinary*,' she said.

Pippa flinched. She did not like the way everyone was bossing Mrs Fudge around today. All her customers were beginning to sound distinctly like Marble Wainwright. However, she made a huge effort to bite her lip and keep quiet.

'And I don't want *her* washing my hair,' continued Coral. 'She's never done it before! I can't have her making a mess of it on such an important day.'

Well, that did it. Pippa felt the anger starting at the base of her skinny feet. It tingled up her legs and settled like a ball of fire in her tummy before it shot out of her head like a rocket. 'I will *not* make a mess of it!' she fumed, her brows locked into an expression of intense fury. 'And I *have* done it before actually. Mrs Fudge has let me practise on her so I know *exactly* what I am doing!'

Coral seemed unaffected by this outburst and simply turned and looked Mrs Fudge up and down as if she had just crawled out from under the carpet. 'Mmm,' she said. 'I thought you were looking a little bit bedraggled today, Mrs Fudge.'

'Huh!' Pippa spluttered. 'If—'

'Pippa dear, that's quite enough. Please go to the kitchen and make a start on the washing-up. *I* will shampoo Coral's hair,' said Mrs Fudge wearily.

Pippa stomped out of the room, causing all the bottles and tubs of lotions and creams and gels to tinkle together. How dare Coral talk to Mrs Fudge like that! Of course the poor old lady was looking 'a bit bedraggled'. She had worked her fingers to the bone to get all her friends and neighbours ready for a party that she herself was not even going to!

She crashed around the kitchen hurling plates and cups into the washing-up bowl and violently squirting in great arcs of washing-up liquid as she turned the taps on full pelt. She muttered loudly under her breath as she cleaned.

'No,' she said eventually. 'I am *not* going to stay in here while Coral says more sneaky, snidey things to Mrs Fudge. I am going back into the salon to protect my friend.'

She crept back in, forcing her face to look meek and mild, even though her tummy was still boiling and churning and all she really wanted to do was to stick her tongue out at Coral as far as it would go and blow the biggest, fattest, meanest, slobberiest raspberry she had ever blown in her life. She took a very deep breath and told herself to smile. (Sometimes this really is the only way to get through a difficult situation.)

Then she said, 'Coral, can I get you anything?'

But now that Coral had had her hair washed and conditioned to within an inch of its very existence she was chattering away to Mrs Fudge like an overexcited sparrow.

'I want Big Hair,' she announced, her arms flailing dangerously to demonstrate exactly what the word 'big' meant. 'Huge, bouncy curls that

 94

swish and shine. Can you do that?'

Mrs Fudge smiled thinly and said, 'You know me, Coral. I always do my best to give the customers what they want.'

Many complaints and restylings later, Coral left Chop 'n' Chat with hair so big Mrs Fudge said to Pippa, 'It'll be a wonder if there's room for anyone else at the party tonight.'

Winston had made himself very comfortable in one of the dog baskets during Coral's overlong appointment and was quite put out at being asked to leave – particularly when he took one look at his owner and whimpered loudly.

At least Winston and Snooks will have something to talk about when they next see each other, Pippa thought grimly. Both their owners are unrecognizable and both their owners have lost the plot of life.

As Coral left, waggling her fingers in what she obviously thought was a chic and sophisticated

gesture of farewell, Mrs Fudge told her to 'be sure to tell us how the party goes'.

Pippa let out a loud and heartfelt sigh. 'Are we done?' she asked, yawning and stretching.

Mrs Fudge nodded and went and turned the sign on the front door to read 'CLOSED'. Then Pippa followed her into the kitchen, where they both fell in an exhausted heap, Mrs Fudge into her favourite worn armchair by the window and Pippa on the window seat.

'My head is sore!' Pippa moaned, rubbing her eyes with her knuckles.

'Oh my goodness, my bunions!' cried Mrs Fudge, closing her eyes as she massaged her toes back to life.

Muffles mewed pitifully and leaped on to Mrs Fudge's lap.

'Poor Muffles,' crooned Mrs Fudge, stroking her sleek grey fur with a free hand. 'You've felt neglected today, I know. We'll have a nice sit-down for a bit and do the tidying later. That's the hardest day we've ever had. I'm sure everyone will give us a break for a few days now.'

10

Pippa Peppercorn Gets
Her Skateboard On

Even Pippa's boring parents had been invited to
the party. But they weren't going. They were too
boring to go to parties. Pippa's dad had picked up
the invitation, sniffed it and said, 'Pooh! Smelly,'
and had gone back to reading his newspaper. Pippa's
mum had glanced at the invitation from over the
top of her book and said, 'Oh dear me, no,' and had
immediately put *her* nose back in her book.

Pippa herself was quite desperate to go. Not
because she wanted to support Trinity Meddler's
new business or because she liked champagne (too
fizzy-poppy and yucky tasting – she'd tried it once
at a wedding when no one was looking), and not
because she wanted to dress up in a 'heavenly' outfit

and chatter nonsense with grown-ups. No, the
reason Pippa wanted to go was because she did not
trust Trinity Meddler one little bit and she wanted to
know exactly what she was up to.

Initially she had toyed with the idea of nicking
her parents' invitation and going to the party in
disguise, but try as she might, she couldn't think of
a disguise that would make her half a metre taller, in
other words adult-size. She'd never been any good
on stilts, and she didn't think you
could get shoes that had heels
that high.

I wouldn't be able to
walk in them anyway, she
reasoned.

She then came up with
the plan of climbing
down from her bedroom
window and sneaking out
to the party. If she got
caught, she would never

be allowed out on her own again, and would most definitely not be allowed to go to Chop 'n' Chat any more, but if she didn't try to creep into the party, she would not know what all the hoo-ha was about and she would lie awake all night wondering.

(And I have to say, if I was her, I would be wondering too. So although what I am about to describe next is possibly not the best plan of action for a ten-and-a-quarter-year-old to carry out on her own, it's what Pippa decided to do, so I'm going to have to tell you about it, even if I don't advise copying her. Which I most definitely do *not*.)

Pippa pulled on a pair of baggy trousers and her bulkiest jumper so that she wouldn't have to change out of her pyjamas. Not the best look for a party, and certainly not a disguise of any sort, but it would mean she could whizz back to bed quickly once she was home. She put on some trainers and tied her hair into a hasty ponytail using a sock, which was the only thing to hand. Then she opened the window and shinned down the drainpipe.

She grabbed her skateboard from the garden shed and tiptoed away from the house before leaping on to it and pushing off down the street at top speed. Her skateboard was a tried and trusted speedy getaway vehicle and she had a feeling she might need such a vehicle that night.

'I know Mrs Fudge said that thing about not crashing gates at parties,' she said to herself, 'but actually I have very good control of my skateboard so I will not be crashing into anything.'

Pippa heard the party before she saw it. The music thudded and thumped through the wet night air, and now that the hoardings had been removed from the front of the building brightly coloured lights streamed out of the new beauty salon into the main shopping street of Crumbly-under-Edge, making birds cower in horror in the branches of the trees.

As Pippa rounded the corner she saw a stream of people entering the building, and through the windows she could make out the silhouettes of guests holding up thin elegant glasses, their mouths

101

wide in laughter. She could have told you who the
people were from the outlines of their hair-dos.
There was Mary with her ridiculous corkscrew
curls – oh, and there was Coral with her Big Hair . . .

Pippa got off her skateboard and hid behind a
nearby tree. The old coffee shop looked nothing
like its former self. In fact, if Pippa hadn't known
better, she would have said that this building had
been beamed in from another planet. The front
door had huge pillars either side like an ancient
temple, and above the door was a flashing sign
which read, in over-the-top swirly letters, 'Heaven
on Earth', and was held up on either side by statues
of angels with shining halos. Guarding the front
door was a big burly man wearing sunglasses,
probably to protect his eyes from all those flashing
lights, thought Pippa. The man was quite similar
to a gorilla Pippa had once seen in a zoo, except
that actually the gorilla had been better-looking.
This man was bald, had no neck and his face was
stuck in the kind of expression people wear when

they are forced to eat spinach before being allowed ice cream. He was talking into a phone, and Pippa strained to catch what he was saying above the pounding music. 'Yeah. No losers, no little girls and no little old ladies. I know that. It's invite only anyway. Trinity said.'

Hmm, Trinity did, did she? thought Pippa.

She scooted silently round to the side of the building, using trees and shrubs as cover, then she picked up a stone and sent it arcing through the air to hit Gorilla-Features smartly on the nose.

'Oi! What's that? You little—!' he cried, looking up. He had assumed the person who had thrown the stone was on the roof. (He wasn't the brightest spark in the socket. Maybe it would have helped if he'd removed those silly sunglasses.)

While Gorilla-Features was distracted Pippa stowed her skateboard behind a bush and tippy-toed as fast as she could to the side of the building. Then she crouched low under a windowsill, squashing herself up tight against the wall.

Gorilla-Features had given up trying to see if there was anyone on the roof and was now muttering, at nobody in particular, 'You'd better not do that again or you'll see the sharp side of my fist.'

Some guard he was turning out to be, Pippa sniggered to herself.

That's when she heard a fakely posh voice she recognized very clearly.

'So what would you advise, Trinity?'

'Well, darling Marble, to start with I think we need to sort out your hair. I'm afraid you can't even BEGIN to think about a makeover until you've chosen exactly the right style to suit you.'

There was a burst of mutterings and sounds of approval from the other guests as they tuned in to what Trinity was saying. There was a high-pitched, 'Yap, yappity-yap!', then Trinity gave a tinkly laugh and said, 'It seems Foo-Foo thinks it's time for a speech!'

The guests agreed and began clamouring:

'Yes! Speech!'

'Hurrah!'

'I love a speech!'

Trinity made some timid remarks along the lines of, 'No, no, really, I was only joking.' But she was soon tapping the side of her champagne flute and clearing her throat loudly to get everyone's attention. 'Very well!' she called out. 'Seeing as you are all so interested in what *dear* Marble was asking me about,' she began simperingly, 'let me take this opportunity to welcome you all and to say that we have been talking Makeovers. The first thing I shall be doing when I open up shop is to invite you all to come and have a free consultation with me. We can discuss your beauty routines, or your make-up, your clothes – anything really. Even your hair. *Especially* your hair,' she added. 'It's all about new products these days, ladies and gents. The old hairdressing methods have gone out of the window. A simple cut 'n' blow-dry just will not cut the mustard any more. I am trained in the most up-to-date hair technology and can advise you on everything from daily haircare to the most modern styling solutions.'

 106

A bubble of excited conversation erupted and filled the room.

Pippa was stiff with shock. Had Trinity Meddler really offered to *style the Crumblies' hair*? Her knees were hurting now from crouching for so long, but she forced herself to stay put so that she could hear what came next.

Foo-Foo started up with his squeaky barking again and the partygoers' chatter faded.

'That's right, everyone!' Trinity raised her voice. 'Heaven on Earth is all about beauty. Whether it's a manicure or a totally New Look, I can do the lot: from top to toe, if that's what you're after. At Heaven on Earth *all* your prayers will be answered! Even your hair-prayers – ha ha! Why not come along on Monday morning and see for yourselves!' And with that she popped a cork from another bottle of champagne and the Crumblies cheered and clapped and whooped and hollered.

I have to warn Mrs Fudge, Pippa realized. Trinity is hatching a plot to take her business away!

107

As she unfolded herself from her uncomfortable position and made her way slowly back to her skateboard, Gorilla-Features shouted, 'Oi!' again. Pippa looked over her shoulder and saw that he was lumbering towards her. 'What you doin' skulkin' about in there?' he roared. 'No little girls allowed!'

Pippa nipped behind the bush, grabbed her skateboard and was off like a greyhound before Gorilla-Features could do anything about it.

She whizzed into her street, zoomed up her garden path, chucked her skateboard under a hedge, shimmied back up the drainpipe and threw herself into bed, pulling the duvet over her. She lay there, listening to her heart pounding in her ears as if she had brought the music from the party home with her. Then, when she was sure all was quiet and no one had followed her, she threw off the duvet, pulled off her jumper and trousers and crawled back into bed to fall into a heavy sleep. The last thing she thought before her dreams took hold of her was, 'This is a disaster waiting to happen.'

11

Sticky Situations

Pippa arrived at Mrs Fudge's the next morning, breathless and full of news about her night-time adventure.

'Missuseff! Missuseff!' she panted, bursting through the door of the salon and sending Muffles scurrying under the washbasins in fright. 'You'll never guess what—'

'Just a second, dear.' Mrs Fudge was at the delicate stage of a particularly challenging haircut that a young man called Kurt had asked for. He had decided to become a punk, and therefore needed a Mohican. The trouble was, his hair was exceedingly fine and floppy, so although the shaving part of the new design had not been a problem, the

getting-the-middle-to-stick-up part was proving
more than an old lady of Mrs Fudge's levels of
energy and patience could muster.

'Make yourself at home. I'm in the middle of
rather a tricky problem,' Mrs Fudge muttered.
'Ooh!' she exclaimed as she gently took her hands
away from the gelled structure only for it to collapse
into a gluey heap once more, leaving Kurt looking
less like a punk and more like a disappointed parrot
caught in a rainstorm.

Pippa sniggered. Finally catching her breath she said, 'Have you tried superglue?'

Mrs Fudge frowned. 'I am not sure Kurt's mother would be pleased if I used superglue in her son's hair,' she said. 'But I do need something extra-sticky . . . Mmm, let me think.'

She pondered her problem, delicately sipping at her cup of tea and daintily crunching into a miniature light-green macaroon. 'Mmm, these macaroons are delicious, though I say so myself!' she exclaimed, her ponderings vanishing as the taste of ground almonds, sugar and pistachio nuts melted on her tongue. 'Have you tried them, Pippa dear? So easy to make, you know – just a question of whipping up some egg whites until they are stiff peaks, rather like  Kurt's favourite hairstyle idea – oh!' Mrs Fudge's right hand flew to cover her mouth.

'What is it?' Pippa asked anxiously. 'Are you choking? Have you got a crumb stuck? Because if you have, I know just what to do. I'll slip my arms around your back like so—'

'No, no!' Mrs Fudge cried, disengaging herself from Pippa's firm embrace. 'I'm fine. Really. It's only that I've had the most ingenious idea!' And she fixed the two surprised young people with her beady blue eyes and said, 'Egg whites!'

Pippa looked confused.

Kurt looked alarmed.

Mrs Fudge chortled. 'Let's try egg whites in your hair, Kurt! It's perfectly natural and easy to wash out. So much better for you than all this horrid gel – and certainly better than superglue!'

So Pippa was sent into the kitchen to fetch a couple of eggs, and Mrs Fudge carefully separated the yolks from the whites and then combed the whites through Kurt's newly dyed bright purple hair. And – hey presto! The most perfect purple Mohican you have ever seen.

Kurt was so chuffed he smiled. Which is not a facial expression which goes with such a haircut, but which nonetheless was very pleasing for Mrs Fudge.

'So,' said Mrs Fudge, 'what was it you wanted to tell me, Pippa?'

'Hmm?' Pippa asked absent-mindedly. She was transfixed by Kurt's new image and was wondering what would happen if she added egg whites to her string-bean plaits. Could she mould them to stick right up in the air like exclamation marks? she wondered.

Mrs Fudge smiled as Kurt paid for his new style and shuffled out of the salon. 'Goodness knows how that

boy's going to sleep tonight!' she joked. 'He'll have to hang his head over the edge of the bed unless he wants to wake up with one of those spikes in his eye. Now, what was it you wanted to say?'

Pippa opened her mouth to speak and then hesitated. Now that she had Mrs Fudge's full attention she wasn't sure she wanted to tell her dear friend what she had overheard the previous night.

So instead she took a deep breath and mumbled vaguely about how she'd sneaked a peak at the party and how packed with people it had been and how glitzy the new beauty parlour looked.

Mrs Fudge sighed. 'Doesn't sound very Crumbly-under-Edge to me,' she said, 'but you can't account for people's taste. Now, dear, help me tidy up in here and then we'll do a spot of baking. We haven't got any more appointments today. I should think everyone's sleeping off the party.'

It seemed that everyone spent the whole of the next week sleeping off the party, as things were very quiet, but by nine o'clock the following Saturday

 114

Mrs Fudge and Pippa were expecting a full house. The bottles of shampoo, conditioner and spray for making hair shiny were arranged in rows with the labels carefully facing outward for ease of reading, the fat little tubs of wax and cream and gel were organized with military precision and the tubes of hair colour were fanned out in a rainbow.

The clock's cuckoo announced itself nine times, popping in and out of the tiny red doors in the clock's face and opening its beak proudly with each chirpy call.

'Nine o'clock,' said Pippa unnecessarily.

The seconds ticked by loudly and accusingly as nine o'clock came and went and the first appointment did not arrive.

'Where is everyone?' Pippa asked, jumping out of the chair and running to press her small upturned nose against the window. 'Marble's usually early.'

'Yes, and it's unlike Mrs Peach to be late,' agreed Mrs Fudge, frowning.

More seconds ticked by in a louder and even more accusatory fashion.

'This is odd,' said Mrs Fudge, tapping the countertop and peering out of the window.

'Maybe there's been an accident,' said Pippa. 'Or maybe they got their times wrong.'

The doorbell remained silent. The phone did not ring. Pippa could hear herself breathing and was sure, if she looked hard enough, that she would be able to see her heart beating.

Muffles had begun circling in front of the salon door and was miaowing rather pitifully.

'Well, they must have forgotten,' Mrs Fudge said eventually, tapping her fingers on the counter again and flicking through her large desk diary with her other hand. 'I will give Mrs Peach a little call. I won't be able to fit her in otherwise – I've got so many other customers booked in for later.'

When Mrs Fudge said this Pippa suddenly had a very, *very* nasty feeling in her tummy. It was the kind of very, *very* nasty feeling she had had in the past when she had eaten something bad like liver and onions or Brussels sprouts (only by mistake, of

 116

course, because what ten-and-a-quarter-year-old would eat such things on purpose?)

She shivered. The yucky churning wobbly sensation would not go away. Pippa took deep breaths and tried to think of lovely things like flying kites and swimming with dolphins (though possibly not at the same time). It was no use. Pippa realized that what she was feeling was fear. Something bad would happen when Mrs Fudge picked up the phone. She should stop her, she should—

Mrs Fudge peered over the top of her shiny steel-rimmed half-moon spectacles as she dialled each number on her bright red old-fashioned phone. She smiled and leaned back against the wall as the dial tone started up.

'Ah, hello? Is that Mrs Peach?' said Mrs Fudge in her twinkliest telephone voice.

Pippa could hear a faint high-pitched gabbling coming from the receiver.

Muffles had stopped circling and was now arching her back, her legs poker straight, her ears flat against her head.

'Ah . . . Ah . . . Ah . . .' said Mrs Fudge, her
rosy cheeks growing paler and paler with each
pronouncement.

Was Mrs Fudge about to produce an enormously
snorty, snotty sneeze? Pippa rushed to her side and
put a hand on her arm reassuringly (but made sure
her face was not within sneezing range, just in case).

'Well, I never,' said Mrs Fudge, shaking her head
slowly as she replaced the receiver.

'Is Mrs Peach sad? Is that why *you're* sad? Cos if it is,
I know just the thing for cheering a sad person up—'

Pippa was babbling and she knew it. But she simply did not want Mrs Fudge to have the chance to say what Pippa feared she was going to. She did anyway . . .

'No, dear. It's not that. Mrs Peach has cancelled.' Mrs Fudge stood up shakily and walked around the counter to stand in front of Pippa. She fixed her with the most serious and unsmiling expression Pippa had ever seen on her dear friend's face. 'It appears we have a rival.'

'A rival?' Pippa repeated, sounding a little like an idiotic parrot.

Muffles hissed.

'Yes, dear. Trinity Meddler is going to do Mrs Peach's hair while she waits for her manicure to dry,' Mrs Fudge replied wearily. 'Never mind. No time for wallowing. Marble is sure to be here soon, so we had better be ready for her, and I think I'll just take a minute to sort out some meringues as well.'

She toddled off into the kitchen, leaving Muffles still hissing, her hackles raised, while Pippa stared blankly at the phone, completely at a loss as to what to do or say.

12

Very Bad News Indeed

At eleven the doorbell rang. Mrs Fudge rushed
to answer it, with Pippa trotting and skipping
nervously behind her.

'Come in, Marble dear!' chirruped Mrs Fudge,
beaming at her customer. 'First things first. How are
you?'

Marble smiled. At least, that's what the pinched
grimace she gave Mrs Fudge was supposed to be.
'I am quite fine, thank you, Semolina. More to the
point, how are *you*?'

Mrs Fudge flushed a deep pink (she did not
like anyone calling her Semolina – would you?)
and stammered, 'I – I'm quite fine too, thank
you for asking. Pippa dear, will you make a

120

fresh pot of tea for Marble?'

'I don't want tea,' Marble said sharply.

Pippa rolled her eyes. She knew she should be grateful that Marble had not cancelled as well, but really, the woman was *such* an old bat!

'Oh, and where's Snooks today?' Mrs Fudge was saying, looking around for the little terrier.

'Snooks?' said Marble carelessly. 'Oh, I left him at home. He was being a pain.'

'Naughty scamp!' smiled Mrs Fudge. 'So, what are we having today then?' she asked encouragingly, sitting Marble down in front of a mirror.

'The thing is, I am utterly *bored* with my hair.' Marble sighed.

'Why don't you buy a wig then?' muttered Pippa.

Marble's eyes twitched to the right suspiciously, but Pippa just looked into the mirror and opened her eyes innocently wide.

Mrs Fudge coughed. 'Right then, Marble. Have you got your scrapbook with you?'

'No. The thing is – well, you *do* know what they

are saying about you, don't you, Semolina?' Marble said suddenly. 'I'm sorry,' she added, not sounding it at all, 'but I believe in the saying "You have to be cruel to be kind".'

'I have never heard of a stupider or more bonkerser saying in my life!' Pippa protested. She rushed to enfold poor Mrs Fudge in her skinny arms. 'Cruelty and kindness are total opposites!'

Mrs Fudge gently unhooked Pippa's hands. 'I – ahem, Pippa, I think we should hear Marble out.'

Marble smiled a smile that was not a very nice smile. In fact, it had 'evil wickedness' written all over it. (Not literally in pen or anything of course, because that would be silly.)

'They are saying that Trinity Meddler's new salon, Heaven on Earth, is "the business" and that you will lose all your customers if you don't shape up a bit and learn some "modern styling solutions". You are, as they say, "so last century".' As she said that last bit, Marble's voice went all singy-songy as though she thought it made her sound young and cool.

Which it most decidedly did not, thought Pippa.

'Ah,' said Mrs Fudge.

'She did a Mohican the other day actually,' said Pippa. 'Isn't that modern enough for you?'

'Pippa . . .' said Mrs Fudge. 'I have to say, *I* feel like a cup of tea myself now – would you be so kind as to run along and make me one? Are you sure we can't tempt you, Marble?'

'No,' said Marble abruptly. 'I won't be stopping. I have been what you might call a little *dissatisfied* with your services of late, so I only really came in today to tell you that I will be trying the *new* salon instead.'

Pippa's mouth fell open and her body ran hot as fire and then cold as ice. Her scalp prickled. I am going to actually explode with anger, into tiny pieces all over the room! she thought. 'How – could – you?' she hissed.

Mrs Fudge laid a cool and careful hand on her thin little arm and said softly, 'If Marble wants to go elsewhere, then that is her decision to make.' Then

123

she looked at Marble and said calmly, 'I only hope you'll be satisfied with your choice, my dear.'

The wrinkled old meanie grimaced. 'Oh, don't you worry about that. The next time you see me, you will not recognize me at all. I will be a New Woman.'

Well, that *would* be nice, thought Pippa.

Things went from bad to worse as poor Mrs Fudge spent the rest of the day receiving phone calls from people ringing to cancel their appointments. Some of them were apologetic, some of them were not, but either way Mrs Fudge's loyal customers had decided one by one to be loyal no longer.

Mrs Fudge sat in her patched armchair with her knitting and looked smaller and older and sadder than Pippa could ever have imagined it was possible for a person to look. Muffles sat in her lap and gave her hand an occasional consoling lick. Pippa did not know what to do with herself at all.

The place is so empty now, she thought as she

 124

looked around the salon. And I do miss Snooks and Winston and all the other pooches.

But what made Pippa really sad was seeing her old friend so disheartened. She tried to cheer Mrs Fudge up by asking her to do *her* hair in a different style.

'I am nearly ten and a half,' she said proudly, 'so maybe it's time to get rid of these.' She held up one of her unfeasibly long red plaits and inspected the tufty end.

'Oh no, dear,' said Mrs Fudge sadly. 'I couldn't cut off your lovely long locks.'

Then Pippa suggested a baking day, but Mrs Fudge pointed out miserably that she didn't have anyone to bake for any more. The suggestion of a sing-song with Mrs Fudge playing along on the banjo was similarly rejected.

'I'm not in a singing sort of mood, I'm afraid,' said Mrs Fudge. 'In fact, if you don't mind, I think I'd like to be left alone with Muffles for a bit.'

At that, Muffles looked rather pleased with herself and uttered a long drawn-out 'Miiaaaooooow', as if to say, 'That's the best idea you've had all day, Mrs Fudge.'

And so Pippa walked sadly out of Chop 'n' Chat into the rain, which she was glad of for once as it went some way to hiding the dirty streaky tear tracks on her pale freckly face.

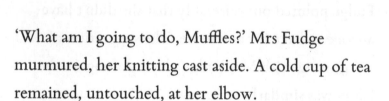

I think it's about time I came along and sorted out this sorry state of affairs.
Don't jump the gun! We're nearly ready for you . . .

'What am I going to do, Muffles?' Mrs Fudge murmured, her knitting cast aside. A cold cup of tea remained, untouched, at her elbow.

The cat opened one eye sleepily and cranked her purring up a notch. She didn't like Mrs Fudge being sad, but she thought she would quickly become used to a peaceful life with no noisy customers. Not to mention noisy dogs.

Just as Muffles was dozing off, the bell to the salon jangled, sending her streaking out of the room in a huff. Mrs Fudge was startled too. A customer after all? she wondered.

But it was Raphael, gliding in as usual. He was smiling, but his eyes were not in it. And as everyone knows, no matter how much effort a person puts into the mouth part of a smile, if the eyes are not smiling too, no one will be fooled for long, particularly someone as wise as old Mrs Fudge.

'Hello, Raphael,' she sighed wearily. 'You look as unhappy as I feel, my dear.'

'Me? Unhappy, darlin'?' Raphael said, his voice a little *too* bright and breezy. 'Nah and never.' He raised his head and sniffed the air like a bloodhound in a rather obvious attempt to change the subject. 'Er, forgive me, Mrs F., but – are you bakin' *anytin'* today?'

Mrs Fudge smiled sadly. 'No,' she said. 'There's no point really. No customers. Deathly quiet, it is.'

'I can believe it, darlin',' said Raphael. 'It be that Heaven on Eart' place. Not so much "heaven" as

127

someting else entirely, if you be askin' me.' Over the last three days, Raphael had gleaned a lot of information about the new salon.

'It's been nothin' but sweet-smellin' gold-edged envelopes from that salon place filled with all kinds o' treats an' promises,' he continued. 'She be sayin', "Come to me salon, darlin's, and I will be makin' you twenty years younger!" And, "Come to me so all your hair-prayers be answered!" Stuff and non-*sense*!' He shook his head irritably. 'She makin' out like she the Fairy Godmother! Well, I is tellin' you, she is more like the Wicked Witch.'

'Raphael dear, there's no point in getting hot and bothered,' Mrs Fudge said quietly. 'The fact is, people like new things.'

Raphael snorted and curled his lip in disgust. 'Cho! New tings?' he cried, slapping the countertop hard. The pens and pencils rattled in their pot and the cash register jangled. 'I'll be givin' them all someting *new* in a minute if they don't all come back to my darlin' Mrs Fudge with their tails between their legs!'

 128

Mrs Fudge couldn't help basking in the warm glow of the postie's fierce loyalty to her and her little business.

'Talking of tails,' she said, suddenly looking thoughtful, 'it's the dogs I'll miss more than their owners, to be perfectly honest with you. And I know Pippa feels the same.'

Raphael nodded wryly. 'I'm with you there, sweetheart,' he said, leaning in conspiratorially. 'I have always said there's more sense between one mutt's ears than in this whole darn town put together!' He slapped the countertop again. 'You should be gettin' yoursel' a little dog for company, you know, if you miss them so much!'

Mrs Fudge shook her head. 'Oh, I don't think Muffles would approve somehow. And anyway, I'm too old to walk a dog. It was lovely to have them as visitors though,' she said wistfully.

'All this talk o' dogs is remindin' me,' Raphael said, lowering his voice and shooting a quick glance over his shoulder, 'I tink I found that woman's weak spot.' His eyes widened knowingly.

Mrs Fudge looked puzzled. 'I'm sorry, dear. I don't understand.'

'That Trinity woman: she don't like dogs!' Raphael hissed.

'No, no, you've got that wrong,' said Mrs Fudge, pushing her spectacles up her nose. 'She has a dog. Rather a sweet little thing called Foo-Foo. I'm surprised you haven't met him. He's her pride and joy. She's very protective of him.'

'Cho! That no dog!' Raphael howled. 'That a *powder puff*!'

Mrs Fudge smiled at Raphael's description of the poodle. 'Now, now, Raphael. I thought you were an animal-lover.'

'I is!' he hooted. 'But that ting is not an-i-mal, I is tellin' you! Have you *seen* it? It is wussy and whoofy and I is tellin' you this, darlin': that pile of fluff has a mean streak, just like its owner. I seen it out in dem streets, growlin' and snarlin' and barin' its fangs at everyting in sight.'

'Hmmm,' said Mrs Fudge. 'It's true that Foo-Foo was a little unsettled when he came here.'

'An' that is not all,' said Raphael, leaning in closer. 'The reason I know that woman don't like dogs is cos she is not letting a single mutt into her salon. When people ask why, she say it cos her "darlin' little Foo-Foo is not to be disturbed".' His voice went up several octaves in an attempt to imitate Trinity. 'And if a person does turn up with their pooch in their arm – she cry! "Boo hoo!"' he sobbed mockingly and wrung his hands dramatically. 'Like it be the end of the world.'

'Raphael, you are naughty!' teased Mrs Fudge. Then she sighed. 'Oh well, maybe my old friends will pop round for a cuppa now and then and bring their pooches too.'

'Maybe,' said the postie, swinging his bag over his shoulder and downing his cup of tea in one noisy slurp. 'But in the meantime I is not lettin' the matter lie, Mrs Fudge my sweetness. Raphael will be bringin' your customers back to you someway, somehow, you mark my words.'

131

13

Dashingly Handsome and Devilishly Clever

Pippa went back to Chop 'n' Chat the next day in spite of Mrs Fudge's request for peace and quiet. It was raining hard, so she skateboarded there in order to dart in and out of the raindrops. (That was what she told herself, but it was really in order to get to Liquorice Drive quicker: she still got soaked, of course.) She let herself in, shook out her raincoat and hung it on her peg, and went straight to the kitchen, calling out, 'Yoo-hoo! It's only me, Mrs Fudge! I've come to see how you . . . oh!'

Mrs Fudge was standing at the kitchen table, a stack of papers in front of her. She was holding one of the pieces of paper in her hands and peering at it through her half-moon spectacles, shaking her head. 'Oh dear, oh dearie me,' she was muttering to herself.

'Mrs Fudge, what *is* the matter?' Pippa said, a note of urgency creeping into her voice. She did not like the way her friend's forehead was looking even more lined than usual.

'I – oh, hello, dear. I . . . oh.' Mrs Fudge fumbled her way to her favourite armchair and sat down heavily, letting the piece of paper fall to the floor.

Pippa darted over and picked it up. It was a bill for shampoos and conditioners and other hairdressing 'sundries' – whatever they were. The bill had the word 'OVERDUE' stamped on it in red ink in angry capital letters.

Pippa felt her throat tighten. She ran to the table and looked at another piece of paper. Another bill. This time from the electricity company, also with red ink and also marked 'OVERDUE'.

'What does this mean?' Pippa asked nervously.

Mrs Fudge looked at her sadly and shrugged. 'It means that the time has come to shut up shop.'

133

'No!' cried Pippa, hands on hips, her red hair lit up like flames from the ceiling light. '*You* are the one who has been doing people's hair for  about sixty years, so *you* are the one who should carry on doing people's hair for about the *next* sixty. Isn't there someone very important in the government we can write to and tell them about Heaven on Earth, so that they can come and close it down?'

Mrs Fudge looked at Pippa. She opened her mouth to speak and then lots of things happened at once.

'I shall retire to a nice little bungalow somewhere—' she began.

'NO!' shouted Pippa.

BANG! A clap of thunder crashed through the

gloom outside and a spear of lightning lit up the salon.

The rain, which had persisted all day, was suddenly cranked up to full throttle, and stair rods of water began hammering against the poor old windows fit to smash them.

Howooool!

'What was that?' Pippa hissed, jumping down from the counter and squeezing next to Mrs Fudge on the saggy old armchair.

'It's a storm, dear,' said Mrs Fudge, shuffling over. There really wasn't room enough for two people and a cat on that chair.

'Well, obviously I know that,' said Pippa, sitting up indignantly, which caused the chair's springs to rattle and groan. 'I have been alive long enough to know what a storm is. There was that one last winter when the cherry tree in our garden came down and—'

Hoowooollll!

'There it is again!' Pippa said. She clutched Mrs Fudge's arm and drew her feet up on to the chair, making herself as small as possible.

Mrs Fudge had been a trifle deaf for a good few years now (which does not mean that she became deaf by eating too many custardy puddings, it just means she was an eensy bit hard of hearing), so she had not noticed the small sound that had frightened Pippa. All she could hear was the pounding rain and the booming thunder and the wittering in her right ear that was Pippa gibbering about a noise that she had 'definitely heard twice now'.

Hoooowwwwwwooooolllll!

Mrs Fudge and Pippa both jumped that time, which was unfortunate as it meant they ended up banging their heads together, and because Pippa's head was full of hairslides and hairgrips and bows and butterfly clips, Mrs Fudge felt as though she had been headbutted by a hedgehog or a bag of knitting needles.

'OUCH!' she cried.

'Sorry!' said Pippa.

Hooooowwwwwwooooollllll!

Mrs Fudge rubbed her head and looked at Pippa questioningly, and Pippa nodded and looked at Mrs Fudge answeringly.

They both got up and crept to the back door and peered out through the glass. It was properly dark now. The kind of wintry late-afternoon darkness that makes you want to light a fire, drink some hot chocolate and watch something daft on the telly. Unless there is a mystery barking noise going on in your back garden, that is, in which case it is the kind of dark which makes you want to bolt all the doors, batten all the hatches (if you have any hatches to batten) and hide under the duvet while your tummy goes bubbly with fear and foreboding.

'Maybe it's one of those Horrible Hounds like you get in Horrible Horror Stories,' Pippa whispered.

'Maybe,' Mrs Fudge agreed. This is all I need, she thought. First I am forced to shut down my salon that I've been running for forty years (not quite sixty, thank you very much, Pippa dear) and now there is a Hound of the Baskervilles looky-likey in my back garden. Except that I don't know if it's a looky-likey as I can't looky even if I likey because it's so *dark*—

CRASH!

Howwwwoooo – oh, for goodness sakes!!

Just at that moment, as if in answer to Mrs Fudge's irritable internal mutterings, a sudden slice of lightning flooded the garden with an eerie white light. And there, on the grass, in the middle of the slice of lightning, as if on-stage under a spotlight waiting to perform a solo, was the smallest, most bedraggled and sorry-for-itself-looking creature Mrs Fudge had ever seen in her whole long life.

Happy now?
BEttEr latE than
NEVEr, I suppose.

It turned its tiny
face towards the window,
hung its head and looked up at them beseechingly

with its large dark eyes.

'Oh, oh, oh!' cried Pippa, all her fears and worries disappearing in a heartbeat. 'It's a dog, Mrs Fudge! A very tiny one. We must let it in!'

'We must,' agreed Mrs Fudge, overcome with pity for the poor little scrap. I wonder whose it is, she thought.

The garden was plunged into darkness again, so Mrs Fudge scrabbled around in a cupboard for a torch. Then, after slipping on her wellies and pulling on her raincoat, she tied a scarf around her snowy-white hair and carefully opened the back door. The wind immediately did its best to wrench the door off its hinges, and Mrs Fudge had to hold on to the handle for blue billy-o to stop herself being whisked off into the night sky. Pippa had her coat and wellies on too by now, so she took hold of Mrs Fudge by the elbow and the two of them put their best foot forward (which, if you really want to know, in both cases happened to be their right one) and ventured forth, bracing themselves against the wind and the rain.

'Where is it?' Pippa shouted above the roar and rage of the storm.

'Where is it?' warbled Mrs Fudge, because if she was a tiny bit deaf when she was sitting in a warm and cosy room, there was no way she could hear a blessed thing out there in that churning, howling weather.

'Woof!' came a plaintive cry.

Pippa gripped Mrs Fudge's arm even harder and steered the old lady towards the sound.

As the torch beam swung round Pippa caught a glimpse of the shivering bundle.

'There!' she exclaimed, and pointed.

Between them, the skinny little girl and the not-so-skinny old lady scooped up the tiny animal and then, turning their backs on the wicked wind, they scurried back to the warmth and dry safety of the salon.

Once inside, with the door carefully closed and bolted, the blinds pulled down and the creature set down on the kitchen floor, Mrs Fudge said, 'My, oh my. You poor, er, thing . . .' she tailed off. She could not tell what kind of a dog he was. He was smaller than

 140

any pooch she had ever laid eyes on. He was smaller even than the next-door neighbour's smallest cat.

'*Charming,*' mumbled the dog. '*I've been called many names in my time, but never have I been called "Thing" before.*'

'Come here,' said Pippa, who had fetched a pile of fluffy towels from the salon and was laying them out on the kitchen table. 'We'll soon have you dry.'

'Oh, he's shivering, the little poppet,' said Mrs Fudge as she carefully patted the dog's soaked and matted fur.

'*Mmmm, I w-w-w-wonder w-w-w-why that is,*' muttered the dog through chattering teeth.

'I think he needs a hot bath and a nice bowl of soup,' said Mrs Fudge.

'*I'd prefer something to sink my teeth into — a juicy rump steak would be perfect — but if soup's all you've got . . .*'

'You run the taps and I'll grab some more towels and maybe a hairdryer, too. Yes, that'll warm him up,' Mrs Fudge said, half to herself and half to Pippa.

They scurried around, busying themselves with

 142

gathering shampoo, soft warm towels and a hairdryer, and as Mrs Fudge was rummaging through the cupboards she came across a dusty old bottle of her late husband's favourite cologne. 'That'll make a nice finishing touch,' she thought, balancing it on the pile of items she had collected together.

Then Pippa very carefully carried the pup up to the bathroom, placed him in the water (which she had, of course, tested first to make sure it was neither too hot nor too cold) and swished in some bubble bath, 'To get rid of the smell of soggy doggy,' she explained.

'*I'll try not to take offence . . .*'

Then once the dog had been scrubbed and rubbed and washed all over with sweet-smelling products (which promised on their labels to make him look 'glossy and shiny and swishy and bright'), Pippa handed him over to Mrs Fudge, who gently blow-dried his fur.

'My, you are a handsome little creature!' she cooed, as the true colour of his coat showed itself. 'He matches your hair, Pippa.'

The dog's fur was as red as a firework, as shiny as

143

a fresh conker and as silky and soft as an expensive scarf. It flicked and swirled in feathery loveliness all over him, and when he shook his head his whole body followed in a rippling wave of glossy beauty. He was peachy, and no mistake.

'I wonder what your name is. No collar . . . ?' Mrs Fudge went on. 'I don't know. People can be so strange. Fancy leaving a perfect pooch like you outside in a storm with no collar and no dog tag. Well, I know what I would call you if you were mine. You look like a miniature dachshund and you're dashingly handsome, so I would call you Dash.'

The minute Mrs Fudge said the name, the little dog fixed her with his liquid-brown chocolate-drop eyes and said, quite clearly, in a deep rich voice as smooth as caramel, 'Thank you. That'll do nicely.'

Afterwards Mrs Fudge would say over and over that you 'could have knocked me down with a feather'. (Although it would have to be a mighty big one, as Mrs Fudge was not exactly what you would call light on her feet. All those cakes, you see . . .)

14

Tricky Trouble and a Soggy Doggy

Mrs Fudge announced she was sorely in need of a good strong cup of tea with extra sugar. 'It's the shock.'

'No,' said Dash. 'It's a sweet tooth.'

Under normal circumstances Pippa would have giggled at the little dog's cheekiness, but these circumstances were decidedly not normal. Indeed, Pippa was so flabbergobsmacked that a little dog was able to be cheeky at all, that instead she said, 'How did you . . . how did you . . . I mean, how did you . . . ?' blinking hard between each stammering statement. She could not bring herself to finish the question, because she could not bring herself to believe that she was *talking to a dog*.

Dash closed his eyes slowly and opened them again with an impatient twitch of his elegant nose. 'How did I arrive in the garden in the middle of a storm? How did I come to be able to talk? How did I grow up to be such a *dashingly* handsome little chap?' he prompted.

'Y-yes,' said Pippa. 'All those things. Except maybe the last one,' she added, thinking, He fancies himself a bit.

'Hmmm,' said Dash, squinting at her through his beautiful dark eyes and lifting his pointy nose in the air disdainfully. 'I heard there was trouble brewing, that a spot of help might be needed. I heard you might be thinking of shutting up shop, Mrs F. And that you, dear Pippa, quite rightly wanted to prevent her from so doing. But if you're going to be like that—'

'Oh, she's not going to be like that!' Mrs Fudge cried, rushing over and stroking Dash's silky ears. 'We're just a little surprised, that's all. Do please tell us how you got here.'

Dash rubbed his head affectionately against Mrs Fudge's plump hand and let out a long and doggy sigh. 'I would have thought that was obvious. I got into the garden through that hole in the hedge that you have been meaning to fix for the past six years.'

Now it was Mrs Fudge's turn to look slightly perturbed, disturbed, puzzled and perplexed. (Her eyebrows went screwy in an attempt to convey quite how discombobulated she actually was.) 'But – but – how in the name of Dickens did you *know* that I've been meaning to fix it? Have you been spying on me? And what about your owners? They'll be worried sick—'

'I take very great offence at your accusing me of *spying*,' Dash snapped. 'It's more a case of keeping my nose to the ground and my ears fully flappy and open. And as for *owners*? Huh! Let me tell you, no one *owns* me.'

He seemed to draw himself up to attention as he said this last bit, like a miniature sergeant major. Pippa half expected him to salute.

147

Instead he gave her a surreptitious little wink and curled his lips in a knowing smile.

Pippa felt her brain whizz and whirr with excitement as the most brilliant thought fizzed and popped and crackled inside her. 'It's like you're some kind of doggy superhero!' she exclaimed, leaping in the hair and pointing at Dash. 'You've turned up like magic just when we need help – and you can . . . you can *talk*!' she added, feeling a bit foolish.

'How right you are,' said Dash, puffing out his little chest and holding his head high. 'I am a bit of a superhero, though I say it myself. Mind you,' he added, arching an eyebrow, 'I only talk to people

who'll listen. And they are few and far between in this crazy world of ours.' He paused, fixed Mrs Fudge with an intense gaze, and then bowed and said, 'I am here, first and foremost, to be of service to *you*, madam.'

Muffles looked down on the scene from her vantage point on the window seat. She lifted her stripy grey-and-white head and narrowed her golden eyes at the little pooch, letting out a low disapproving hiss. She very much doubted a dog could be of service to anyone.

Mrs Fudge gave a little chuckle, in spite of her sadness. It was lovely to have a dog in her home again (even if he was a bit full of himself). 'I have to say, that's the most welcome news I've had in days,' she said. 'So how *are* you going to help me save my salon?' she asked. She had quickly got over the realization that she was talking to a dog. Somehow Dash was so confident he made it feel as though it was the most natural thing in the world. And besides, she reminded herself, she had encountered far stranger things during her travels with Mr Fudge, all those years ago.

The little dachshund trotted over and rubbed a velvet-soft ear affectionately against the old lady's leg. 'If I might make a suggestion?' he asked.

'Go on,' said Mrs Fudge, intrigued.

But they were interrupted by Raphael, who chose that moment to put his head round the salon door, making everyone jump a little as they had all been concentrating so hard on what Dash had to say.

'Hello, darlin's! I didn't mean to scarify you, but with all that splashin' o' rain and crashin' o' thunder I figured you didn't hear me call hello and you certain sure didn't hear me ring de bell, and when I hear voices, I tink to myself, "I jus' go right in as normal." And here I is, come to see how *you* is, sweetness.' Raphael finished.

Pippa looked expectantly from Dash to Raphael and back again. Would the postie be one of those 'people who'll listen'?

'Oh my! And who is this gorgeous little fella?'

Raphael said, stooping down to Dash's height. He cautiously stroked the little dog's glossy coat, before scooping him up with one huge hand and tickling him under his floppy feathery ears. 'What's his name?'

'Dash,' said Dash and Mrs Fudge in unison.

Raphael let out a rumbling belly laugh and his eyes sparkled. 'My! Did you hear that, lady? He answered!'

'He did,' said Mrs Fudge simply.

Raphael roared with laughter. 'I never did hear o' such a ting!' he cried. 'You are a marvel!'

Dash held his head high and said proudly, 'So I'm told.'

'He's more than that, he's a superhero!' Pippa chattered excitedly. 'And he's come to save Mrs Fudge's salon from that horrible old—'

'Quite, dear,' cut in Mrs Fudge.

'At least you has taste in dogs, Mrs F.,' Raphael said as he stroked Dash's smooth coat. 'This is a *real* dog, not like dat silly little ball o' white fluff.'

151

'Which silly ball of fluff are you talking about?' Dash said, pricking up his ears.

'That poodle. Foo-Foo-Foodle or whatever the blazes he called,' Raphael snorted.

'Foo-Foo's the dog at the new salon,' Pippa explained. 'The salon that's taken all of OUR business,' she added sourly.

'Ah.' Dash nodded, listening intently.

'Have you *seen* what Trinity does with it? Sweetness, I is tellin' you, that not a dog. That a pussycat!' He roared with laughter again.

Dash let out a short sharp bark. 'That's some insult!' he said, and dodged a vicious sideswipe from Muffles.

Pippa sniggered.

'As if it wasn't bad enough she call it that stupid name,' Raphael continued, 'now it have pink ribbons in it hair, and she give it a man-i-cure! Manicure for a dog!'

Pippa was about to join in the merriment when she felt her brain give a jolt. She had a strange

152

sensation that it was working independently of her and instead of letting her laugh with Raphael and joke along with him about the silly poodle, it was sending out other messages, that flashed and whirled and demanded to be read and acted upon at once.

Manicures – dogs – ribbons in its hair – hair – dogs . . .

'Mrs Fudge!' Pippa cried, leaping up and down on the spot and clapping her hands. 'I've got it! I've got it! Oh, thank you, Raphael, thank you! You are a complete superstar and I love you!' she yelled, throwing her arms around him and hugging him tight.

'Hey, sister, watch out!' he laughed, teetering backwards on his Rollerblades. 'You have me falling on me backside if you not careful!'

Luckily Raphael was an expert rollerblader and was used to dodging cars and dogs and cats and people walking around with their headphones on, not looking where they were going, so he regained his balance and steadied himself.

'Now you calm down, Pippa girl, and tell us what

this is about,' he said, holding her still while she
continued to hop about as if her pants were on fire.

Pippa pointed at Dash and tried to speak, but her
words would not come out in the right order. 'He
shampooed and we gardened him and found and
now he's beautiful!' she babbled.

'What are you on about?' Dash asked irritably,
quite perplexed by the spectacle he had just

witnessed. He carefully put some distance between himself and the bouncy girl and excitable postman, seeking out a dog basket and curling himself tightly into it.

'You know you said it was the dogs you missed more than the people now that – now that Chop 'n' Chat is . . . well, you know,' she tailed off uncomfortably.

'Yes, dear,' Mrs Fudge replied, nodding encouragingly.

'Well, you don't need to be missing out on dogs.'

'No, she won't,' Dash agreed. 'She's got me now and I'm going to solve all her problems.'

Mrs Fudge patted his head.

Pippa pressed on. 'That's *exactly* what you're going to do, Dash! You and everyone else's dogs! Because you're going to open a completely new business, Mrs Fudge – just for dogs!'

Raphael had been watching Pippa carefully as she spoke, his heavy black eyebrows knitted together in deep concentration. As Pippa said her last few words,

155

his eyebrows sprang apart as if they had been released by an elastic band, and he banged his fist on the kitchen table. 'Girl, you is so right!'

'Perhaps you two would care to illuminate us further?' Dash asked.

Pippa looked at Raphael, and Raphael winked at Pippa. They both grinned and announced in unison:

'A pooch-pampering parlour!'

'A — a what?' Mrs Fudge faltered.

'A WHAT?' Dash barked crossly.

Pippa clapped her hands and her crystal-blue eyes shone with happiness. 'Yes! A pooch-pampering parlour! All those people with dogs getting muddy and soaking wet in this terrible stormy weather we've been having. You did it for Dash, and look how handsome he is now!'

'I think you'll find that that has more to do with my own personal beauty actually,' Dash muttered.

'Hallelujah, sister!' declared Raphael, throwing his long skinny arms up in the air and causing Muffles to scuttle under Mrs Fudge's chair in alarm.

 156

'Pippa, darlin', you is a gen-i-us! This is exactly what the town is needin' right now. You said yourself the Crumblies' heads have been turned by something new, Mrs Fudge! Well, a pooch-pampering parlour will be the best new thing this town has seen yet,' Raphael said. 'Pippa, you is cookin' on gas, me darlin'!'

15

A Simply Splendid Solution

Suddenly Mrs Fudge and Pippa and Raphael were all talking at once, none of them listening to the others.

'Oh, this is going to be fantastic!' Pippa was saying. She was pirouetting around the kitchen, her stringy plaits whirling around her head like a windmill. She chattered breathlessly as she spun round and round.

'You have most of the equipment you need already. And the dogs are already at home at Chop 'n' Chat – they've been coming here with their owners for years.'

'I could even start baking little snacks for the dogs instead of just buying in treats,' Mrs Fudge was saying dreamily. 'Oh, why didn't I think of this before?'

'What a fuss. Anyone could have told you that was the perfect solution,' Dash muttered, secretly very cross that he himself had not been the orchestrator of this undoubtedly marvellous plan.

'Let me go and tell the Crumblies now! Right away!' begged Raphael. 'And if you want to make leaflets to advertise, I can deliver dem!'

'What about making some pretty cards to post through people's doors or some posters to put up around the town?' Mrs Fudge suggested, her brow creasing. She was thinking of the gold-edged invitations and promotional offers that Trinity had used to wow her new customers.

'I've got a much better idea,' said Pippa. 'Dash can be our very own real-life advertisement.'

'Charming – volunteer my services without my

159

say-so, why don't you?' Dash grumbled, lifting his head slowly from his cushion-like position in the corner. 'What happened to me as superhero, I'd like to know . . .'

Mrs Fudge's eyes sparkled with amusement, but she went over to the little dog and patted him gently on the head, whispering, 'My dear Dash, let's just hear what Pippa has to say.'

Dash softened at the tenderness in her voice and answered quietly, 'Just as you like, Mrs F.'

Pippa beamed and said, 'You, Dash, are the perfect walking example of the wonders Mrs Fudge can do to a pooch in need of pampering!' Dash looked a little offended but did not interrupt. She went on, 'You look sooooo beautiful with your coat all glossy and shiny and your ears all flappy and feathery and your tail all waggy and wonderful.' At these words Dash bowed his head in humble agreement. 'So I think we could go around town showing all the Crumblies what a marvellous example of poochy perfection you are, and I will tell everyone that Mrs

 160

Fudge was the one who made you look this way, er, even better than usual.'

'I can get you a megaphone, darlin',' said Raphael. 'I got the one we used for the fête last summer at the town hall – remember?'

'Wonderful!' said Mrs Fudge, clapping her hands. Her face was fully restored to its former rosy-cheeked glory and her eyes were twinkling again.

Dash was the only one to look rather subdued. 'I have to admit it is a wonderful idea and I am only sorry I did not think of it myself. Particularly as I came here on a rescue mission to help you, Mrs F.'

Mrs Fudge consoled him. 'But don't you see, dear,' she said kindly, 'it *is* all down to you. If you hadn't come in from the rain like you did, well, then you wouldn't still be here now. And if you weren't still here now, Raphael would not have met you and seen what a handsome creature you are.' At this, Dash became most bashful, and if it was possible for a russet-coated dachshund to blush, then he would have done. 'And then –' Mrs Fudge paused for maximum effect and to make sure all her compliments had well and truly sunk in – 'none of this would have come up in conversation at all. So you see, you are our own personal superhero, dear.'

Dash lowered his head and looked up at Mrs Fudge gratefully from under his long dark eyelashes. 'I do see what you are saying. Thank you.'

'Only one ting you haven't thought of,' said Raphael. 'What is you going to call youself?'

'In my opinion, young Pippa would be the person to ask,' Dash suggested humbly. 'She is very imaginative, and being, er, perhaps more in touch with the youth of today, if you don't mind my saying so, she might possibly have some ideas that

would appeal to a wider audience.'

Mrs Fudge shook her head and smiled. 'Cheeky pup!' she scolded playfully.

Pippa needed no more encouragement and began scribbling names down on a large sheet of paper in her enormous loopy handwriting – and crossing each one out again when Dash objected to it.

'What about something fun like "Soggy Doggies"?' she suggested, her eyes gleaming.

'*Not* very flattering,' Dash muttered.

'O-kay,' Pippa said slowly drawing a line through the idea. 'How about "Pretty Pups"?'

'Too feminine,' said Dash.

Another line went across the page.

'"Marvellous Mutts"?'

'A bit insulting, if you don't mind my saying so.'

Pippa crossly scratched the words out and began tapping her foot impatiently. '"Handsome Hounds", then?'

Dash lowered his head modestly. 'That's more like it.'

'I don't know,' said Mrs Fudge. 'I think that leaves out the lady dogs, actually.'

Pippa let forth a great huff of frustration and stood up quickly, pushing back her chair. She put her hands on her hips. Then a light came on in her eyes again and a sparkling grin illuminated her face and she put one finger up in the air and cried, 'I've got it!' She cleared her throat, stood tall and with a sweep of one long skinny arm she declared, '"Mrs Fudge's Pooch-Pampering Parlour"!'

'By Jove, I think she's got it,' said Dash, running round and round Pippa's feet in crazy excitable circles and yapping wildly.

Mrs Fudge beamed.

Raphael clapped his hands. 'That be it!'

Mrs Fudge's eyes were shining with emotion. 'I've said it before and I'll say it again: I don't know what I would do without you, Pippa Peppercorn.'

16

Mrs Fudge's Pooch-Pampering Parlour

So the following afternoon after school, a small
skinny girl with red plaits was to be seen zipping
around the streets of Crumbly-under-Edge on
a skateboard with a russet-coloured miniature
long-haired dachshund running beside her, his

feathery-fine ears flapping happily behind him. And if you had been in the vicinity, you would have heard the following words bellowed out from a megaphone and carried along on the breeze:

Roll up! Roll up!
Come to Mrs Fudge's Pooch-Pampering Parlour!
You like to be pampered – what about your dog?
Dogs need pampering too!
Don't delay! Book today!
Come to Mrs Fudge's to give your dog a treat.

People stopped in the street and pointed and commented on the cheery little girl with her friendly freckled face and the gorgeous little dog at her heels. And they chattered and gossiped and agreed that a pooch-pampering parlour seemed like a marvellous idea and vowed to call and make a booking as soon as they got home.

Pippa grinned to herself as she scooted through the town and bent down to pat Dash on the head

saying, 'You're the business, Dash!'

'Let's hope so, for Mrs Fudge's sake,' he replied.

The two new friends were so caught up in the excitement of the venture that they didn't notice a tall, dark, slinky figure standing in the doorway of a garishly over-decorated building. The figure curled her lip in distaste as Pippa and Dash went by and bent to pat the white fluffy head of her own dog. 'I give them a week, Foo-Foo,' she said sourly. 'Just one week, and those smiles on their silly faces will have completely disappeared.'

'Yap, yappity-yap, yap!' came the squeaky reply.

Mrs Fudge had not been idle while Pippa and Dash had been doing their rounds. She had been concocting special recipes for dog biscuits and had invested in a bone-shaped biscuit cutter. 'I must make sure my new customers are treated as well as my old ones,' she told Dash later. 'And *you* deserve a treat yourself after all the running around you've done!'

Dash gratefully gobbled up a tasty cheese-flavoured biscuit bone and delivered his verdict: 'Absolutely delicious, Mrs F.! You know, you should develop a sideline and sell these. I'm sure you'll soon have the phone ringing off the hook.'

And would you believe it? (You probably won't, but it's honestly true.) The minute he said that, the phone actually rang!

Dash scurried back and forth yapping, 'This is it! This will be your first customer!' Pippa had to grab him and whisper to him to be quiet.

Mrs Fudge shot her a nervous smile, then picking up the phone slowly and deliberately, she said, 'Hello, Mrs Fudge's Pooch-Pampering Parlour!'

Pippa let out a snort of excited laughter and pinched her nose sharply to stop herself from having hysterics.

Mrs Fudge was saying, 'Hmm? Yes, I see. Well, do bring him in. How does tomorrow sound?'

At last she put the phone down, grinning all over her kindly face, and said, 'We have our work

cut out for us today. I will need—'

'Who was it?' Pippa butted in. She knew it was rude to interrupt, but she was bursting to know who had called.

Mrs Fudge's grin faltered for a split second and then she said brightly, 'Marble!' She shrugged as Pippa rolled her eyes to the heavens. 'She wants Snooks to come for a shampoo and "general tidy-up".'

'Why does it have to be Marble?' groaned Pippa. 'I bet she's got a stash of dog-grooming magazines she wants to show us. She'll have the most ridiculous ideas for poor Snooks.'

But there was no time for Mrs Fudge to comment as the phone rang again. And again. And again. Mrs Fudge scribbled away, taking down more and more bookings, her cheeks growing rosier and her eyes more twinkly by the hour.

Mrs Fudge's Pooch-Pampering Parlour was open for business at last!

*

Marble arrived for her appointment bang on time.

That is, Pippa assumed the woman on the doorstep was Marble, but to begin with she couldn't be sure. She opened the door, a toothy grin on her face (not because she wanted to be friendly to Marble, you understand, but because she was bubbling over with happiness at being Mrs Fudge's assistant again). However, when the customer turned to face her, Pippa's smile faltered. The woman had long spidery eyelashes that seemed to be growing out of her eyelids like some strange black weed; her jet-black glossy hair was cut into a jaw-length bob so sharp you might have cut your fingers on it, and her make-up . . . well, 'dramatic' would be the least unkind way to describe it. Her cheekbones were highlighted with sweeps of dark pink, her lips were stained a deep purple, and her fingernails, which were long and perfectly manicured, had been painted to match. The overall effect was quite alarming, and if it hadn't been for the fact that the person was short and dumpy instead of tall and willowy, Pippa would

170

have sworn in front of a judge and jury that she was actually face to face with Trinity Meddler.

She must have stood gawping with her mouth hanging open for a full sixty seconds before the woman spoke. 'Well, are we going to stand here all day or are you going to let me in?' she squawked, barging into the hall.

Pippa stumbled back. This was Marble, all right. As she passed, a strong perfume filled the air. Pippa had a vague memory of having smelt it somewhere before, but she was so confused by now that she could not put her finger on where or when that was. She took hold of Snooks's lead, grateful that it was for his benefit Marble had come, and took advantage of that fact to spend a bit of time talking to him instead of having to pass comment on his owner's bizarre new looks.

'Hello, Snooksie!' she cooed, rubbing his tousled head. 'It's *so* nice to see you again.'

Dash appeared in the corridor. 'My word, what a scruff-bag,' he yelped.

Snooks growled menacingly and strained at the leash.

'Bad manners too, I see,' said Dash, and swiftly scampered back into the salon.

Shame I can't understand what you said to Dash, Pippa thought, looking at Snooks with amusement.

'Are you going to take my coat then?' Marble huffed.

Pippa stared at her coolly and said, 'If you'd like to hang it on the peg, Marble, I'll take Snooks in for *his* appointment.' Without waiting for an answer, she walked the little Welsh terrier into the salon.

'Humpf,' said Marble, tossing around her newly glossy hair. 'Is this *really* a dog-grooming business? Looks exactly the same as when I last came here.'

'Hello, Marble,' said Mrs Fudge lightly. 'I see you've had rather an impressive, er, makeover.'

Marble fluttered her ridiculously long eyelashes. Pippa hoped they would fall off and get stuck to her enormous bosom.

'Oh, do you like it?' Marble simpered. 'Trinity

 172

really is an inspiration, you know.'

'*Is* she?' said Mrs Fudge with a touch of sarcasm.

'Oh yes. All those years chasing the perfect look –
you know, I was never satisfied,' Marble said cattily,
'but all it took was one visit to Trinity and she knew
exactly what I wanted the minute I walked through
the door.'

'I bet she did,' Pippa muttered under her breath.

'What is going on?' Dash growled, rubbing
his head against Pippa's shins. 'I sense a certain
atmosphere in the room.'

Pippa bent down and whispered, 'Marble's a bit
of a nutcase, that's all.' She was glad Marble didn't
appear to be one of those 'people who'll listen' when
it came to hearing Dash speak.

Mrs Fudge had turned her attention to Snooks.
She lifted him on to one of the twirly-whirly chairs
and stroked him gently. 'So, what would you like me
to do for Snooks, Marble?'

Marble smiled sourly, reached into her outsized
shopping bag and pulled out a stack of magazines.

173

Pippa had to force herself not to groan out loud. 'I'll go and put the kettle on, shall I?' she said hastily, desperate to escape before she said something rude.

'Yes, dear,' said Mrs Fudge, shooting her an amused look. 'And bring some of those special biscuits, can you?'

Marble had heaved the pile of magazines on to the counter by the till and was flicking through the pictures, stabbing at images of heavily groomed dogs.

'Now that I have achieved a certain level of sophistication in my own grooming,' she said, 'Trinity has hinted that I should look to other areas of my life. I must admit I think she's right. I mean, look at *her*. She is a woman with taste. Her dog, Foo-Foo, never has a hair out of place, and consequently they look so good together. Whereas Snooks here – well, frankly, I feel he is letting me down, and Trinity agrees. That's why she lent me these magazines. Foo-Foo has done some of the modelling for them, as it happens.'

Dash let out a funny whining noise and barked,

'Well, fancy that! Well done, Foo-Foo.'

Mrs Fudge glanced at him sharply.

Snooks began barking excitedly at the interesting smells now coming from the kitchen. His nose twitched eagerly in the air and his tail flicked animatedly from side to side as Pippa emerged with a tray of Mrs Fudge's dog biscuits.

Marble's eyes lit up. 'Is this a new recipe, Semolina?' she asked, greedily reaching out her hand.

Mrs Fudge flinched at being called by the name she so despised – why did Marble insist on using it? – then her mouth twisted into a mischievous grin. 'Yes, you could say that,' she said, as Marble grabbed a handful and popped a couple into her mouth.

'Hmm,' Marble said, chewing hard and swallowing with some difficulty. 'Er, interesting.'

Pippa then threw a biscuit to Dash and one to Snooks, who gobbled them up appreciatively.

Marble watched the dogs and said, 'I would stick to giving them to the dogs if I were you.'

Mrs Fudge winked at Pippa and said, 'Good idea, Marble. Now, you were showing me those magazines?'

'Yes. Aren't they gorgeous?' Marble proceeded to point out her favourite images.

Pippa's eyes boggled at the photos of dogs in embroidered jackets, dogs in sweaters with gold and silver printed on them, dogs in hats, dogs in sunglasses and dogs with diamanté collars and

anklets to match. Some of them had even had their claws painted red or pink or orange.

'Er, Marble,' said Mrs Fudge when she could take no more. 'These dogs are all poodles.'

'Yes, thank you, Semolina,' said Marble insolently. 'I can see that.'

'But, er, Snooks is a Welsh terrier,' Mrs Fudge continued, as if talking to someone with only half a brain. She looked helplessly at the lovable wiry bundle of fun sitting on the twirly-whirly chair in front of her and took in his shaggy eyebrows and his lolling pink tongue, his messy grey-and-brown coat and his woolly paws. 'I can't make Snooks look like these poodles, I'm afraid, Marble,' she said. 'It just wouldn't be right.'

Marble flared her nostrils angrily and put her hands on her wide hips. She pouted her purple lips and said, 'I thought the customer was *always* right? That's what you used to say. It's what Trinity says too. Call yourself a pooch-pampering parlour? Well, I must admit Trinity did laugh when she heard about your new business venture. It's not as if you know anything about dog-grooming, is it? Come on, Snooks. Time to leave.'

Pippa felt sure that if Mrs Fudge had not been there to stop her she would have picked up the teapot and poured the entire contents over Marble's silly glossy head. But instead she whispered to Dash, 'What are we going to do? We can't let her leave! She'll tell the whole town that Mrs Fudge is rubbish, and the pooch-pampering idea will be over before it's even started!'

'Leave this to me,' said Dash. He scampered over to Snooks and snuffled into his ear. Pippa realized he was whispering.

Snooks immediately sat down hard on the floor and refused to be moved. Marble was pulling at him, trying to pick him up, but he would not budge. She put his lead back on and tried dragging him forcefully out of the room. It was no good. Her dog had become a dead weight.

'It seems,' said Mrs Fudge, a playful twinkle in her

eye, 'that Snooks would like to stay.'

'Oh, very well,' Marble huffed and puffed. She had become rather sweaty in her attempts to remove her dog from the parlour and her make-up was beginning to smudge. She let go of Snooks and said crossly, 'Trinity says he needs a good wash and scrub-up, so if nothing else you could do that for him.'

Mrs Fudge simply raised her eyebrows at these ungracious words and proceeded to busy herself with the task at hand. She asked Pippa to hold Snooks while she shampooed him with the new minty dog shampoo she had bought. Then she swiftly whispered to Dash that he should explain to Snooks what was going on so that he would stay calm. Once the dog was washed, Mrs Fudge sat him under the hood of one of the huge hairdryers while Pippa fed him treats and talked to him. To finish off, Mrs Fudge clipped his claws, trimmed his wiry coat and tidied up his eyebrows. A spritz of Mr Fudge's old cologne was used as a finishing touch.

'You're the neatest, sprucest Welsh terrier I've ever seen,' said Dash approvingly.

Snooks wagged his tail enthusiastically and gave a short sharp bark.

Dash looked up at Pippa. 'One happy customer,' he said.

'I was wondering,' said Pippa, as she watched Marble very reluctantly handing over the payment to Mrs Fudge. 'You said Trinity thought you should smarten up all areas of your life. Why would *she* not give Snooks a makeover?'

Mrs Fudge looked up quickly to see Marble squirming. 'I, er, I don't know,' she said lamely.

'Oh, only I notice that Foo-Foo is, as you say, very well groomed. Where does she take him?' Pippa persisted.

Marble was at a loss for words. Finally she shook her head. 'Dunno,' she muttered. 'Anyway, I've got to go. I have an appointment to have my toes waxed,' she said, changing the subject hastily as she moved towards the door. 'We can

 180

let ourselves out. Goodbye.'

She broke into a funny little trotting run and was gone in a blink. Which is probably a good thing, as Pippa was doing a rather dramatic impression of being sick and saying hoarsely, 'I do NOT want to even THINK about Marble's hairy toes, thank you!'

And neither, I am sure, do you.

17

Business Is Booming

'You are *so* clever, Mrs Fudge!' Coral twittered, arriving with Winston straining and panting. His huge tongue was drooping out of his slobbery jaws. 'I don't know *why* no one's ever thought of this before. After all, there are *so* many dogs in Crumbly-under-Edge.'

Winston was sniffing the floor like a wrinkly, furry vacuum cleaner. He had always liked the niffs and whiffs in Mrs Fudge's place, but today his little tail was whirring round and round in circles like a helicopter blade; he looked just about ready to take off.

'My word, what on earth has got Winston so excited?' Coral said, gasping as she tried to pull her

dog back to heel. 'Anyone would think he'd never been in here before.'

'Maybe it's the smells of the new products I've bought,' suggested Mrs Fudge. 'I could hardly carry on with the same shampoos as before – the ones I used on my human customers, before they all . . . you know, well, that is . . .' she faltered, suddenly embarrassed as she realized what she was about to say.

'Oh yes, I've been meaning to explain,' Coral said, colour rising in her cheeks. 'I – I am sorry I haven't been coming here to have my hair done—'

'It's a bit late for that,' Pippa grumbled. But under her breath.

Mrs Fudge waved a hand dismissively at Coral. 'What's done is done,' she said. 'No use crying over spilt milk, as my granny used to say – or indeed spilt shampoo, ha ha! Now that I have branched out into catering for the local canine community's needs, no more needs to be said on the matter.'

'Oh good!' Coral let out a tinkly laugh. 'Shampoo

under the bridge, shall we say?'

'Hmm,' said Mrs Fudge. (She was thinking that was enough of the hairdressing puns, and I agree with her.)

Winston suddenly barked loudly, causing everyone to jump and then turn to see what had caught his attention.

'Woof, yourself,' said a voice.

'Oh, Dash,' said Mrs Fudge. 'You didn't half give us all a fright!'

Winston gave a yelp and strained on his lead in Dash's direction, causing Coral to yelp too as she was dragged across the floor by her dog. Pippa couldn't tell from the expression on the pug's face whether he wanted to flatten Dash or lick him to death. The dachshund was clearly glad the pug was on a lead and took advantage of the situation to slowly and deliberately wash his paws. Muffles had taken up a new position on the countertop, as far out of reach of all visiting dogs (and Dash) as possible, and could be heard hissing faintly at the kerfuffle below her.

 184

'Who is that?' Coral asked breathlessly as Winston gave an extra-strong tug on his lead.

'This,' Mrs Fudge answered, scooping up Dash despite his protestations – 'Do you mind? I was in the middle of washing!' – '. . . is Dash. He has recently come to live with me.'

'How lovely!' Coral panted. 'What a good idea to get a dog as a companion after . . . after . . .' she faltered again.

'Yes, quite,' said Mrs Fudge hastily. 'Anyway, I don't think we want him distracting us now, do we?' she said pointedly, and she put the dachshund down, giving him a stern look.

'Charming!' he declared, but Winston chose that moment to let out a particularly terrifying snarl, and so he flicked his ears as carelessly as he could and trotted off quickly, calling out, 'I had things to do anyway,' before bolting from the salon so that Mrs Fudge could shut the door behind him.

Muffles yawned extravagantly and stretched on the countertop, as if to say, 'One gone, one to go.'

185

Winston let out a disappointed whimper, which even though Mrs Fudge could not have translated directly she was pretty sure meant, 'Blast, I nearly had that little dog.'

Coral took a deep breath and wiped her forehead with the back of her hand. 'Winston, you are being a very naughty boy,' she said weakly. 'I hope you're going to behave now for Mrs Fudge.'

Mrs Fudge had her apron on and was busy sorting through numerous sparkling bottles on one of the shelves. Pippa had firmly tethered Winston to a bar on the wall which Raphael had fixed up for the purpose of restraining dogs that were too large or too frisky to go into one of the basins or on one of the twirly-whirly chairs. She set to work vigorously washing Winston and covering him in a minty-scented shampoo.

'Winston's a very well-cared-for dog,' Mrs Fudge said to Coral, while Pippa rubbed and scrubbed. 'I'm sure he doesn't need much attention. Once he's washed, should I look at his claws

 186

perhaps? They might need clipping.'

Coral nodded enthusiastically. 'And I thought maybe we could give him some little accessories,' she twinkled.

'Acc-accessories?' Mrs Fudge stammered. 'He's a pug. I'm not sure—'

'Oh, all the best pooches are accessorized to match their owners these days,' Coral simpered, patting and preening her own shimmering locks. Pippa looked up at Coral's alarmingly bright red hair and nails and winced. 'I was thinking maybe Winnie would look nice in . . . something . . . red,' Coral finished lamely.

Mrs Fudge looked uncomfortable. 'If you're thinking of what Ms Meddler has done with her dog—'

'Foo-Foo! That's right,' Coral butted in enthusiastically. 'Have you seen the adorable darling lately? He's had his nails – I mean claws – done in a wonderful shimmery purple, and when it's particularly chilly out Trinity puts him in the most adorable purple coat.'

He wouldn't need one if she didn't shave his fur off round his middle, thought Pippa.

'Ye-es,' said Mrs Fudge. 'I – I'm not sure that what goes for poodles goes for pugs, if you get my meaning.'

Pippa stifled a giggle as an image of Winston in a bright red coat with claws to match filled her brain. It would be like dressing a great hulking rugby player in ballet shoes and a tutu!

Mrs Fudge sighed. All the time she had been a hairdresser she had lived by the saying 'The customer is always right', because she had learned from experience that people would not be told any different, even if what they were asking for was quite frankly ridiculous.

'Very well, Coral. I'll see what I can do. We'll stick with washing and brushing Winston for today, and I'll trim his claws. I'll let you know if I can get hold of any, ah, accessories that I think would suit him.'

★

Mrs Fudge's appointments diary for the pooch-pampering parlour was soon booked up every day from nine in the morning until it closed at five in the evening. Mrs Fudge needed Pippa's help every afternoon, and they would have found it all exhausting if they hadn't been having so much fun. When they weren't clipping, washing, drying or titivating the pooches' fur, they were making pots of tea, baking cakes and dog biscuits and chatting with their old friends and neighbours.

The only thing that dampened their spirits was the fact that Trinity Meddler's name was never far from anyone's lips.

'She has filled the Crumblies' heads with such nonsense!' Mrs Fudge said at the end of a particularly long Friday of primping and pampering every kind of dog from the smallest chihuahua to the largest Great Dane, all of which, according to their owners, had to be accessorized and decorated to within an inch of their poor lives.

'They are all frankly *such* a rabble,' said Dash

smoothly. He was curled up on the window seat in the kitchen, his feathery tail tucked softly around him like a velvet draught excluder. 'And I'm sorry to say this, Mrs Fudge, but most of the dogs have left here looking more than a little ridiculous. I mean, tying a large silk ribbon around that wolfhound's neck! What on earth was his poor owner thinking? I feel I ought to speak out on behalf of all canines.'

Muffles gave a 'miaow'.

'You see? Even the cat agrees with me,' said Dash.

'I know, dear,' said Mrs Fudge, sipping her tea. 'Nonetheless, it is good to be busy again.' She sighed contentedly. 'It's as if we never had that quiet patch, isn't it, Pippa dear?'

Don't you dare laugh

Mrs Fudge's kitchen was as cosy as it had been on Pippa's

190

first day at Chop 'n' Chat. A Victoria sponge was rising in the oven while a fresh batch of homemade dog biscuits cooled on a rack; Mrs Fudge had kicked her shoes off and had her stockinged feet up on a footstool as she relaxed in her armchair.

Pippa was sitting on the floor, sipping at a glass of lemon squash and flicking her feet back and forth impatiently. She was ravenously hungry after all the rushing around in the salon that afternoon and could not wait to sink her teeth into a slice of the sponge cake. She was about to say as much when an entirely different thought popped into her head.

'Mrs Fudge,' she said, 'do you realize that almost everyone who has a dog has been to see us – but not *quite* everyone?'

'What's that, dear?' Mrs Fudge had been dozing off. She started at the sound of Pippa's voice, blinking rapidly and pretending she had not been asleep at all.

'Not everyone has made an appointment,' Pippa said.

191

Dash lifted his head, stretched and yawned. 'So?' he said lazily.

'Well, I think it's a bit odd that the most pampered pooch in town has not come here to be pampered, that's all,' Pippa said.

Dash cocked one ear and suddenly looked alert, his dark eyes shining. 'Are you referring to the ball of white fluff Raphael was talking about?'

Pippa giggled. 'Foo-Foo. Yes,' she said.

'Trinity must look after him herself, surely? He always looks incredibly, er, well-groomed to me,' said Mrs Fudge generously. ('Well-groomed' in this case being code for 'downright ridiculous'.)

Not for the first time, Pippa felt a warm glow spread through her as she looked at the little old lady. She wondered how she could be so kind about the person who had taken so much away from her.

As if reading Pippa's mind, Dash said, 'You are a marvel, Mrs Fudge. Most other people would be very bitter about what Trinity has done.'

Mrs Fudge went a light shade of pink and

muttered something inaudible. But Pippa rushed in to support her as usual, saying, 'But that's just it, Dash. Mrs Fudge is *not* most other people.'

Mrs Fudge waved a hand dismissively. 'If truth be told, I'm not really all that upset any more about Chop 'n' Chat. I've always preferred dogs to people – present human company excepted, of course,' she added hastily, 'and I would never say as much to my friends and neighbours, but dogs are so much easier to please, wouldn't you say, Dash dear?'

The little dachshund wagged his feathery tail appreciatively and nuzzled Mrs Fudge with his wet nose. 'You are so right,' he murmured.

Pippa rolled her eyes.

'And if you think about it,' Mrs Fudge went on, warming to her theme, 'I have a lot to thank Trinity Meddler for.'

'Oh?' Pippa said.

'Yes, dear. If she hadn't come and taken my hairdressing business away from me, I would never have opened the pooch parlour,' Mrs Fudge said pleasantly.

Dash agreed enthusiastically. 'Nor would you have met me,' he said, a little mysteriously.

'Now that would have been a shame!' said Mrs Fudge, her eyes twinkling.

Pippa nodded. All in all, it did seem as though things had turned out rather well.

18

Doggy Disappearances

And the story might well have ended there. Except
that, luckily for you, dear reader, it doesn't. But
for some of the people *in* this story it is not lucky
at all, because the very next day a dramatic disaster
occurred that sent the Crumblies into a whirl and
had Mrs Fudge worrying about her business all over
again.

It was Mrs Prim who raised the alarm. She came
rushing into the pooch-pampering parlour at nine
o'clock, having booked her spaniel, George, for a
brush and a claw trim. She looked very flustered,
her shiny new Heaven on Earth hairstyle looking
less 'heavenly' and more 'dragged-through-the fire-
pit-of-hellish'. Indeed, apart from the fact that she

195

certainly was in a state, she looked more like the old Mrs Prim, Pippa thought, which in some ways was strangely comforting. But all such thoughts disappeared immediately when Pippa held out her hand to take George's lead and saw that Mrs Prim had come without her dog.

'Hello,' said Pippa. 'I think you've forgotten something, Mrs Prim. Where is George?'

'Oh, Pippa, that's just it! I don't know! I was hoping you might have seen him,' she cried, clasping her hands together. 'He must have run away, but I can't think why. He's never done it before. And I told him we were coming here, and he was *so* looking forward to it – I could tell.' Poor Mrs Prim's eyes filled with tears and her bottom lip began to wobble dangerously.

Pippa was a girl who was made extremely uncomfortable by the sight of anyone crying and she most definitely did not want to witness Mrs Prim sobbing her heart out. For a start, she would be bound to make the most horrendous noise, and for a finish, all that make-up she had recently taken to plastering over her face would surely run and make a hideous mess. She managed to say kindly but firmly, 'You sit down and I'll fetch Mrs Fudge. She'll know what to do.'

Mrs Fudge came into the salon with Dash hot on her heels and demanded to know where and when George had last been seen.

'I put him in the hall in his basket last night and locked the house as usual, and when I came down this morning he was g-g-g-oooonnnnne!' Mrs Prim wailed.

'Don't worry,' said Dash. 'The poor fool won't have gone far. He's not exactly the brightest bulb in the box.'

Pippa sniggered.

'I don't know what you're laughing at, young lady,' Mrs Prim snapped. 'You would be laughing on the other side of your face if it was *your* dog who was missing.'

'I don't think I would,' Pippa said, frowning. 'I

197

don't think I could laugh on the other side of my face because I haven't got a mouth there—'

'Pippa . . .' Mrs Fudge said in a low voice.

'What?'

Mrs Fudge raised her eyebrows and flicked her head in Mrs Prim's direction. The woman was sniffing loudly and blowing her nose into a handkerchief so large you could have used it as a tablecloth if it hadn't been so covered in snot and tears and make-up.

'Oh, yes. Sorry – I wasn't laughing at you anyway,' Pippa said. 'I was just – oh, never mind. Dash here is super-duper at sniffing things out. He's a bit of an all-round superhero in fact! We could come round to yours and do a bit of detecting. I'm sure we'll track George down.'

And so Dash, Pippa and Mrs Fudge followed Mrs Prim back to her house. But they didn't get very far, for on the way they met Coral, who was also weeping and wailing and blowing into a huge handkerchief.

 198

'It's Winston!' she cried. 'When I came down this morning to give him his breakfast—'

'He wasn't there,' Pippa finished.

'Yes!' Coral exclaimed. 'I mean, no! I mean – how did you know?'

Pippa turned to Mrs Fudge, who was grim-faced. 'This cannot be a coincidence,' she said.

'What do you mean, "a coincidence"?' Coral twittered. 'What's going on? Do you know something?'

Pippa shook her head. 'No, but Mrs Prim's dog is missing too. We were just going to help her look for him.'

'Listen, Coral dear,' said Mrs Fudge, laying a consoling hand on her neighbour's arm. 'Why don't you and Mrs Prim go home and wait in case your darling dogs turn up. Pippa, Dash and I will ask around the town, and we'll get Raphael to keep his eyes open for anything suspicious too.'

The two ladies tearfully agreed that this was most probably the best plan of action. They traipsed off,

199

arm-in-arm, both dabbing at their faces with their
hankies. Once they were safely out of earshot, Dash
piped up.

'Mrs Fudge,' he said, 'may I suggest that you
too go back home and wait by the phone? Pippa,
why don't you make up some posters and we can
ask Raphael to distribute them. Meanwhile, I will

do some sniffing around. We will meet back at Mrs Fudge's later today.'

Mrs Fudge nodded, but Pippa said, 'I'll make posters later if I have to, but right now I want to help look for George and Winston.' She was secretly a bit cross with Dash for taking over.

Mrs Fudge agreed and put a stop to Dash's protestations. 'Two brains are better than one,' she pointed out wisely. And Dash could not think of anything to say against that.

Now, although Dash was not a bloodhound and had not been trained in tracking a scent, he had what all dogs have: a very sensitive (although small) snout. He also had complete confidence in his ability to use this nifty nose of his to sniff out anything he asked it to. And so he set off for Mrs Prim's house, nostrils to the fore (and indeed the floor), and made a mental note of everything he discovered on his way. Pippa came with him, to offer her assistance in interpreting any evidence Dash turned up.

Mrs Prim was looking out of the window when they arrived and opened the front door as they came up the path.

'Come in,' she said, her face overshadowed with worry. 'Go wherever you like, but I'm not sure you'll find any clues. The house looks just the same as it ever did, apart from the fact that dear George has gone,' she whimpered. 'I'll stay by the phone and keep a look out of the window.'

Dash and Pippa made their way carefully around the house.

'What can you find?' Pippa asked.

Dash glared at her. 'I may have superhero powers, but I do need more than ten seconds in the house to use them to full effect,' he snapped.

Pippa pulled a face, but said nothing.

'Hmm,' muttered Dash, his nose to the ground. 'Someone's been eating biscuits.'

'Not surprising,' said Pippa. 'Mrs Prim is well-known for her biscuit addiction.'

'All right, what about this – nail-varnish remover!'

 **202**

'She's been having manicures at Trinity's,' Pippa pointed out. 'Like everyone else around here,' she added bitterly.

'O-kay, how about coffee granules?'

'Mrs Prim drinks a lot of coffee with her biscuits,' Pippa said helpfully.

Dash stopped sniffing and sat back on his haunches. He fixed Pippa with a particularly firm glare. 'I really appreciate your help,' he said, in a tone that suggested he didn't at all, 'but are you perhaps suggesting that Mrs Prim kidnapped her own dog?'

Pippa pulled a face. 'I don't know. You're the one who's supposed to be brilliant at sniffing out clues. All I'm saying is, you haven't sniffed one out yet. All those smells you've mentioned are to do with Mrs Prim. You need to find something that *isn't* to do with her. And seeing as I know her better than you do, you need my help.'

Dash wrinkled his doggy forehead in concentrated thought. Then he sniffed the front door and said,

'Perfume. A very distinctive scent with strong cinnamon top notes,' he added.

Pippa curled her lip. 'Top *notes*?' she said disbelievingly. 'What are you talking about?'

Dash raised one doggy eyebrow. 'Scent is a complex and many-layered thing, my dear. A "top note" is the element of a smell that comes to the nose first. Sniff for yourself,' he said, gesturing to the door. 'It is most apparent on the door handle.'

Pippa bent down and breathed in the air around the handle. 'Smells kind of door handle-y,' she said, wrinkling her freckled nose in disgust. 'Can't say I could pick out any *top* notes. Or *bottom* or *middle* ones for that matter,' she added sarcastically.

Dash flicked his silky soft ears. 'Which is why *I* am the nose of this operation. And the brains, *for that matter*,' he said, sprinkling on a smattering of sarcasm himself. 'Let's hope I have enough brains for the two of us.'

Pippa let out a frustrated gush of air and crossed her skinny arms firmly across her chest. 'If you're

 204

going to be like that, perhaps I should leave you to it,' she said.

Dash trotted up to her and rubbed his head against her legs in a conciliatory gesture. It might have been ticklish if she hadn't been wearing such thick woolly tights. 'Why don't you take me to Coral's house? We need to see if there are similar signs there.'

'We'll be off now, Mrs Prim!' Pippa called, sticking her head around the sitting-room door.

'Any clues?' Mrs Prim asked eagerly.

Dash surreptitiously brushed up against Pippa and uttered a low growl: 'Don't say anything yet.'

'Er, not sure really,' said Pippa. 'We're going to Coral's now to see what we find there. We'll let you know.'

Off they went, Dash's nose to the ground, Pippa's eyes sharply peeled for clues. Dash sifted through the everyday smells of Crumbly-under-Edge: rubbish and food and the bottom of people's feet and fumes from buses and cars. Once at Coral's house, however, the same cinnamony pong rose clearly above the other smells.

'Well, I think that nails it,' he said, licking his fur in a very pleased-with-himself manner. 'The person responsible for the dog-napping has an extremely distinctive cinnamon scent, so all we have to do now is follow that scent from the two properties and we will track down the culprit . . .'

Pippa would say afterwards that she had already had her suspicions about Dash's self-professed superpowers and that she had not thought much of the way Dash had undertaken the task of tracking down the criminal. But even so, she was not prepared to hear Dash, having led her a merry dance around the streets of Crumbly-under-Edge, his nose firmly to the ground the whole way, look up at last and say simply, 'Oh.'

'"Oh", indeed,' said Pippa, tapping her foot angrily (a foot that was quite sore by now, after following Dash everywhere – as indeed was her other foot, for she had not hopped all the way round).

The two of them looked up and then looked

at each other. Dash would have blushed with embarrassment if he could have done. As it was, he merely glanced down at his front paws bashfully and coughed. 'Ahem, it would seem we have ended up—'

'Back where we started!' Pippa cut in, her voice raised in exasperation. 'So much for you having the sharpest snout in the south, the best beak in the business, the handiest hooter ever heard of!' she exclaimed. 'You are one hundred per cent useless, Dash. We are back at square one, with no more idea of who took the dogs than how marshmallows are made or how you get jam into the middle of a doughnut.'

'Well, if you want to know that, I'm sure I can tell you—' Dash said.

'NO!' Pippa shouted. 'I want you to solve the mystery of the missing dogs!' And she proceeded to complain about what a waste of time his 'so-called detective work' had been so far and that 'if he thought he was impressing her, he had another think coming' and—

Dash set about nibbling at something caught between his claws on his left paw. He let Pippa go on and on until she had run out of things to rant about, and then he let his paw drop and said calmly, 'There is no need to get in a stew. Every problem has a solution; it just so happens that his problem is a particularly knotty one and will take more mulling over. It is what I like to call a two-bone problem.'

'A *two-bone* problem?' Pippa repeated. 'What on earth is that?'

'It simply means,' said Dash with infinite patience, 'that I need to sit in *peace and quiet* —' he put much emphasis on these three words — 'and think the matter through. And to ensure that I concentrate all my efforts on this, it would help immensely if you could procure two juicy bones for me to gnaw on. Helps to focus the mind, you know.'

'The cheek!' Pippa declared. 'First you drag me all over town for nothing, and now you're demanding bones! Normally a dog gets a juicy bone as a *reward* when it's already done something clever.'

Dash sighed and lay down in the middle of the path. 'Just as you wish,' he said carelessly. 'I'll have a snooze instead then. I am very tired after all the traipsing around I've done for you this morning.'

'For *me*?' Pippa was getting really quite angry now. 'We're doing this together for Mrs Fudge and her neighbours, and you know that. If we don't help to find the dogs, then she'll have lost two of her customers for good. And how do we know that other dogs won't go missing too? Just think what that would mean!'

Dash put his head on one side and looked puzzled. 'What would it mean?'

Pippa gave him a thunderous look, took a deep breath and said angrily, 'There will be no pooch pampering if there are no pooches to pamper – that's what it would mean!'

19

Detective Dash Is on the Case

Dash got his two bones in the end, after he remarked coolly that without his help Pippa really would be in a pickle, 'And that would not help Mrs Fudge either now, would it?' He proceeded to gnaw and nibble at them with great gusto. It wasn't a particularly nice sight to behold, and involved a lot of cracking and crunching which made Pippa and Mrs Fudge quite uncomfortable, so they retired to the kitchen to share a pot of tea and a slice or two of chocolate cake.

'I don't know,' said Mrs Fudge, dabbing at her lips with a napkin. 'Life has been very strange lately.'

Pippa finished a mouthful of cake, nodding furiously. 'I bet Trinity Meddler's behind this mystery of the disappearing dogs.'

'What on earth makes you say that? She's nothing to gain by it,' Mrs Fudge said.

It was true, Trinity's business was going well without her having to worry about what Mrs Fudge was up to.

'In any case, dear,' Mrs Fudge pointed out, 'she doesn't like other people's dogs being around her poodle, Foo-Foo, remember, so why would she want to kidnap any?'

'S'pose,' Pippa said reluctantly. She left Mrs Fudge and went out to check on Dash to see if his bone-crunching had given him any inspiration. So much for focusing the mind! she thought. The 'two-bone problem' nonsense was just an excuse to get a couple of treats out of us. And now he's snoring, the little rotter.

Dash opened one eye, and as if reading her thoughts said, 'Give me five more minutes and I'll be recharged and ready to go.'

'You haven't worked anything out, have you?' Pippa asked accusingly.

211

Dash was silent.

Pippa toyed with telling Dash exactly what she thought of his so-called superhero status, but then told herself he was the only help she had at present. So she swallowed her annoyance and said, 'OK, well, we are going to have to go and see Mrs Prim and Coral and tell them that we can't find their dogs. Their reactions are not going to be pretty,' she added with a grimace.

Pippa grabbed her skateboard and whizzed down the lane to Mrs Prim's with Dash hot on her wheels. A familiar short, squat figure came into view up ahead.

'Oh no, it's Marble,' Pippa hissed. 'Quick, let's turn back.'

But Dash had stopped and was sniffing the air greedily. 'No, no, wait. It's that perfume again. Can you smell it?'

Pippa lifted her head and opened her nostrils wide to inhale the air. At first all she could make out was the metallic smell of the rain rising up from

 212

the sopping wet ground, but then there was a hint of something else. Something very familiar. It was a little bit like the aroma of Mrs Fudge's fruit slices, only slightly sharper. 'Yes, I think so,' she replied.

'It's the cinnamon again,' yapped Dash. 'And unless I'm much mistaken, it's coming from Marble. Follow me.'

They followed Marble at a safe distance, ducking behind trees and bushes and scooting down alleyways. They need not have worried however; Marble was in a world of her own, humming to herself and clutching a bundle of something to her large chest.

'What if she's got George and Winston in there?' Pippa whispered.

'I hardly think so,' said Dash snootily, with a haughty swish of his tail.

'Why not?' Pippa asked, her voice rising in indignation.

'Elementary,' said Dash. 'They are rather large and wriggly dogs. She would not be able to carry them both at the same time.'

Pippa was sulking now. 'Humpf,' she said. Who did this little dog think he was with his 'two-bone problems' and his 'elementaries'? Although Dash was right of course, she admitted to herself. Not many people could have coped with carrying George or Winston very far, particularly not tubby Marble Wainwright.

Then Pippa had a thought. 'If they're too difficult to carry, the person who took them must have *lured* them out of the house somehow. And I know those dogs. The only thing that would make them leave their comfy homes is food.'

'Well done, Detective Pippa,' said Dash patronizingly. 'So are you going to tell me who did the luring?'

They managed to lose sight of Marble they were arguing so much. But then, on rounding a corner, they came face to face with her. She was sitting on a bench with the bundle, which looked like a purple blanket, resting on her lap.

 214

'Oh, er, fancy meeting you like this,' Pippa blurted out. She blushed and shuffled her feet.

Dash rolled his eyes, but said nothing.

'Er, Marble,' Pippa began cautiously. 'Did you know that Mrs Prim and Coral have lost their dogs?'

'No,' said Marble sharply. 'Why on earth would I know that?'

'Just asking,' said Pippa. 'I suppose Snooks is all right, is he? Only he'd normally be out walking with you, wouldn't he?' Now that Pippa was up close, she could detect a spicy smell that seemed to be coming from the blanket.

'Snooks?' Marble repeated stupidly. 'Oh, Snooks!' she said, as though remembering something from her dim and distant past. 'Yes, he, er, he got a bit fed up and, er, he wandered off. A couple of days ago actually. But it doesn't matter,' she finished carelessly.

Pippa was struck dumb. She glared at Marble uncomprehendingly. How could anyone be so mean about their own dog, especially one as cute as Snooks?

215

Dash had noticed something and was nudging Pippa's leg with his wet nose. 'Pippa,' he said urgently, 'look!'

Pippa shook herself out of her cloud of bewilderment and followed Dash's gaze. The bundle on Marble's lap had begun to wriggle and Marble was fussing over it, cooing and jiggling it and making baby noises. Then there was a final tussle and a small white face with a twitching pink nose and two gleaming black eyes appeared from the blanket.

'A poodle?' Pippa and Dash exclaimed.

Coochie coochie cooooo!

'Yes,' Marble said, hugging the quivering white creature close to her large bosom and beaming. 'This is Woofsie.'

'Woofsie?' Pippa and Dash chorused in unison.

'Yes, Woofsie, my new little darling,' said Marble. She glared at Dash. 'Could you please keep your hound quiet? All that yapping will frighten my little poppet.'

'Yapping? Poppet?' said Dash.

Pippa gave him a meaningful glance (the meaning was 'She can't understand you like I can, remember?').

Dash looked unabashed. 'Serves her right for being so stupid,' he said.

'Er, Marble . . .' Pippa began hesitatingly, 'what's going on?'

'Nothing,' said Marble stubbornly.

Pippa blinked and coughed and said croakily, 'I don't understand.'

Marble gave a sudden tinkly laugh. 'It's all about poodles these days, don't you know? Darling Trinity

217

found me this one. They are so much easier to accessorize than Welsh terriers. You know, although it pains me to say it, Mrs Fudge was right about that. And the best thing is, I can get Woofsie pampered while I'm having my own treatments done – whoops!' Her hand flew to her mouth as she said this.

'What?' Pippa cried in horror. 'You mean . . . ?' She couldn't finish her sentence.

'Woofsie is having his treatments done at Trinity's salon,' explained Dash unnecessarily.

Marble of course did not hear what Dash had said, but she looked sufficiently guilty nonetheless. She hurriedly covered Woofsie in a blanket and said, 'I have to go. It's time for Woofsie's lunch.'

And with that, she got up from the bench and hurried off, glancing once over her shoulder to see if Pippa and Dash were following.

20

Oodles of Poodles!

Pippa scooted slowly and glumly back to Mrs Fudge's. Dash tried to distract her with a constant stream of what he considered to be intellectual conversation, but which Pippa considered to be a lot of hot air and nonsense that was getting in the way of her thinking.

Questions and niggles were wriggling round and round inside her brain until she felt as though her head was full of ants.

What is Marble doing with a poodle? she wondered as she glided along, staring at the pavement before her and doing her best to block out Dash's witterings.

It was as she thought the word 'poodle' that she

looked up and saw . . . a poodle. It was so startling to see her thought translated into reality that Pippa wondered for a moment if she wasn't perhaps dreaming, but she glanced down at Dash and saw he was still there, trotting along beside her. When Pippa looked up again, the strangest scene was unfolding before her eyes.

She had reached the newest part of Crumbly-under-Edge, where each house was brightly painted with bold, contrasting colours and had a closely trimmed lawn at the front. Each of these lawns was divided from the next by a neat picket fence, and walking on these lawns and in and out of these houses, were people. Ordinary people, the like of which Pippa saw every day of her life. Except that on this day there was something very *un*ordinary about them. Something unsettling. Something downright freaky.

Every single one of them had, in his or her arms, or walking along beside them . . . a white, fluffy, furry POODLE!

 220

Pippa prodded Dash.

'And so, if I were you, I'd—'

'Dash! Dash!' she said through gritted teeth. 'Stop talking and LOOK!'

Dash huffed in irritation at being interrupted in mid-flow, but then looked up as he was asked. The sight ruffled even his neatly brushed fur.

'Oh my!' he yelped quietly. 'Let's get out of here. I don't feel safe – what if it's me next?'

Pippa nodded urgently. She bent down to pick Dash up so that they could make a speedy getaway, but as they turned to make their way back to Liquorice Drive they came face to face with Coral, who was cradling an armful of white fluff and beaming from ear to ear like a child on Christmas morning. The little dog peered at Pippa and Dash with its glassy black eyes and cocked its small woolly ears.

'Hello, Pippa dear!'

Pippa and Dash looked at the bundle in Coral's arms and both swallowed hard.

'*Another* poodle?' Pippa said, horrified. 'But . . . how? Why?'

The poodle bared its tiny sharp teeth and let out a low growl.

'Trinity,' said Coral. 'When I told her all about Winston going missing, she seemed so *genuinely* upset about it. She even had tears in her eyes. She's *such* a sweetie.' She sighed. 'And of course I was devastated. But it's obvious he's not coming back. So when darling Trinity told me that poodles were all the rage and said she could get me one for a reasonable price, I thought, "Why not?" – which is how I came to be the proud owner of Popsie here. And the truly marvellous thing is—'

'Don't tell me,' said Pippa. 'You can get the two of you done for the price of one – at "darling Trinity's"!'

'Yes,' said Coral, looking puzzled and rather hurt at having the wind taken out of her sails. 'How did you know?'

Dash had been making a series of strange low

223

murmuring sounds, aimed in the direction of the poodle. The poodle had been growling more and more menacingly and now erupted into a volley of high-pitched yapping.

'Come on, Dash,' Pippa shouted over the noise, not caring how weird she looked, talking to the dachshund as if he was human. 'We've got to get to the bottom of this.'

'The bottom of what?' Coral called out after them. 'Oh, Popsie, shush now,' she added, patting the poodle's head.

But Pippa did not turn round to answer. She wanted to put as much distance between herself and Coral as quickly as she could so that she could have a proper conversation with Dash before they had to deliver this latest bit of bad news to Mrs Fudge.

They reached the park and Pippa flopped on to a swing, keeping a firm hold on Dash so that they could talk quietly with no passers-by noticing.

'So,' she said, once she had caught her breath, 'what did that poodle have to say for itself?'

224

'I'm sorry,' said Dash, wriggling to free himself from Pippa's suffocating embrace. 'What do you mean? And could you stop squashing me like that? All you had to do was ask, and I would have settled on your lap with no fuss at all.'

'Sorr-eee,' Pippa said, with mock patience. She loosened her grip and allowed Dash to make himself comfortable. After much going round in circles on Pippa's knees to find 'exactly the right spot', Dash at last settled down and curled his tail neatly around him.

Pippa began to speak quietly. 'You are a dog, right?'

'How very well observed.'

She ignored him. 'You are a dog, and you can *speak* dog, whereas I am a human and for some crazy reason I can understand *only* you, not any other dog. So I was wondering if you could please tell me what Coral's poodle was saying just then? I don't know – maybe it has some idea about what's happened to Snooks and Winston and George.'

225

Dash let slip a bark of laughter.

'And what exactly is so funny?' Pippa fumed. 'I can't see that there's anything to laugh about. Three dogs are missing, and random poodles keep turning up in their place. For all I know, Mrs Prim might already have a poodle to replace George as well. It's dreadful! Don't you have a heart? I thought you were supposed to be a superhero, come to solve all our problems, but if anything, things have gone from bad to worse since you arrived!'

Dash looked suitably ashamed, but Pippa was sure the corners of his mouth were still turned up in a cheeky little smile. 'I'm sorry,' he said quietly. 'It's just, the very idea of a poodle having anything interesting or useful to say!' His voice ended in a squeak.

Pippa gritted her teeth in irritation.

Dash wiped his eye with his paw. 'Sorry,' he said again. 'The short answer to your question is that the poodle did not reveal any useful information.'

 226

'But did you ask any *useful* questions?' Pippa persisted crossly.

It was Dash's turn to look annoyed. 'Of course I did. What do you take me for? I am a professional detective and I am taking this investigation very seriously. I asked where they had all come from, for a start. It merely told me what you already know: that they came from Trinity's.'

'But *before* that?' Pippa insisted.

'They can't remember,' Dash said simply.

Pippa groaned. 'I don't believe it.'

'Well, you're going to have to. That's always the problem with poodles. Their heads are so full of fluff, they cannot keep hold of a thought from one moment to the next.'

Pippa scowled. 'I think that is a very spiteful thing to say,' she said.

'No more spiteful than the things you have said about Marble – or indeed about Trinity Meddler,' the little dog pointed out. Pippa blushed, because she knew it was true. 'Look, I know it seems harsh, but poodles are simply not the brightest matches in the box. If you could ask any other dog, they would agree. Poodles are very cute to look at, even I can see that. But they are not known for their brain power, are they? In fact, it doesn't surprise me at all that Trinity is the one who has introduced them into the town. If ever there was a human who was just like a poodle, it's her.'

Pippa felt a switch flick in her brain as the little dog said this. 'You are a genius, Dash,' she said, her crystal-blue eyes flashing with excitement.

'I know,' Dash said modestly.

Pippa chose to ignore this, grabbing him and hoisting him up to face her. She looked straight into his eyes and said, 'Trinity is only interested in appearances, right?'

'Right,' said Dash. 'But I don't see—'

'Listen,' said Pippa. 'What did Trinity do the minute she arrived in this town? She took away all Mrs Fudge's clients and finished her hairdressing business once and for all. OK? So then what

 **228**

happens? You arrive and we get the idea for the pooch-pampering parlour, and people start coming back to Mrs Fudge's. Right?'

'Right, but I still don't see where this is going . . .'

Pippa blew at her fringe in exasperation and threw her hands in the air. 'It's obvious! Trinity wasn't letting people bring their dogs into Heaven on Earth because she said they upset her darling Foo-Foo, so they decided to bring them to see Mrs Fudge, didn't they?'

Dash coughed and tossed his head importantly. 'Ah, yes — so you are suggesting that Ms Meddler grew jealous and set out to sabotage Mrs Fudge's new business venture.'

'Eh?' said Pippa.

Dash growled. 'Trinity had already got the whole town dressing and behaving like her, but that wasn't enough. She became jealous when they went back to Mrs Fudge's to have their dogs groomed. It can't be a coincidence that everyone has a poodle now.'

'Exactly,' said Pippa. 'Trinity is definitely behind the mystery of the lost dogs. Question is, how do we prove it?'

21

Into the Poodle's Lair

By the end of that week, it became clear that
the only dog it was acceptable to be seen with in
Crumbly-under-Edge was a poodle. Even Mrs Prim
had replaced her lovely spaniel, George. She was
seen out walking, a poodle in her handbag, and was
proudly telling anyone would who listen that she
'simply adored her darling Mr Fluff', as she had
named the poor creature.

Mrs Fudge tried to remain chirpy, saying, 'At
least they'll make good customers. Poodles are funny
creatures and they certainly need a lot of grooming.
Just wait – I'm sure my customers will soon be
calling up to make hundreds of appointments.'

Pippa could not bear to tell Mrs Fudge about the

latest 'two for one' offer of Trinity's. 'It's like a nasty spell has been cast on the Crumblies,' she exclaimed. 'No one cares a bean about where their old dogs are! How come everyone suddenly wants to be like Trinity? Has she hypnotized people, do you think?'

Dash emitted a low growl of impatience. 'If she had, do you not think we would have got a good dose of it too?' he snapped.

'Eh?' Pippa said.

Dash let out a long sigh and put his head on one side, letting one of his luxuriant feathery ears flop on to the pavement. 'I mean, if Trinity had hypnotized the people of this town, do you not think that *we* would have been included in her hypnotism, in which case we would not be feeling at all suspicious of her?'

'Well, what *is* going on then?' Pippa threw her hands in the air in complete exasperation. 'Even *you* don't seem to care any more, Mrs Fudge!' she said.

'My dear!' protested Mrs Fudge, 'I most certainly

do care. But what can we do, other than what you and Dash are already doing? Namely, looking out for clues and asking around. And in the end,' she pointed out, 'the dogs that are missing are not our responsibility. They are not our pets. If their owners don't want to find them, well, I can't see how we can interfere.'

Pippa was fizzling with anger.

And to make matters worse, just as she had predicted, the townsfolk did begin to desert Mrs Fudge once again – in droves. In favour of Heaven on Earth.

Whereas Trinity had always maintained that dogs such as Snooks and George and Winston 'upset her Foo-Foo terribly', it seemed that *poodles* were more than welcome to enter her establishment. She even went so far as to offer customers the alarming option of having their poodles *dyed* to match their outfits, and soon queues of people with their poodles filled her salon, waiting to be transformed.

The town, Pippa thought, had quickly become a nightmarish place to live. Even Kurt had been seen leaving Heaven on Earth with a blue poodle, the fur on its head gelled to a miniature spike – a replica of Kurt's own Mohican.

It would not be long before Pippa and Mrs Fudge and Raphael were the only normal-looking people left and Dash was the only normal dog.

'There must be some way of shocking people into seeing what they've become,' Pippa said. 'Maybe they will only notice if I can prove what a baddie that Trinity is. And what about you, Dash?' Pippa began to sound panicky. 'Maybe you're not safe while there's a dog-napper on the loose?'

Dash was in his basket by the stove, quietly

gnawing a bone. 'Hmm,' he said, in between chews. 'Don't worry about me. I've always been able to look after myself. However, I do think we need to investigate Heaven on Earth more closely. Pippa, why don't you make an appointment for yourself and while you're there you can ask some questions?'

'Me? An appointment?' She snorted very indignantly. 'I am not setting foot in that place. It would be disloyal. And anyway, Trinity will say that I need to "ask my mummy for permission".'

Mrs Fudge smiled. 'I think Dash is on to something actually. You go and distract her by having something done to your hair – I'll call and let her know you're coming. She won't throw away an opportunity to get herself a new customer. Dash can slip in with you and maybe pick up a few clues.'

Pippa's heart was very heavy in her chest. 'I really don't want to go into that place at all,' she said, shaking her head, 'but I suppose I don't have much of a choice. Come on then, Dash – let's get it over and done with.'

She gathered Dash into her arms and they set off on Pippa's skateboard, with the wind at their backs and Dash's ears flapping in the breeze. 'Put me down before she sees me,' he said, as they approached the gaudy, over-decorated building of Heaven on Earth.

But as Pippa bent to set the little dog down on the pavement Trinity appeared in the doorway of her salon. 'Too late,' Dash muttered and leaped inside Pippa's red duffel coat.

'Pippa Peppercorn!' Trinity cooed, walking down the steps, her poodle skulking behind her. 'Mrs Fudge called to let me know you were coming. I've got half an hour free before Marble comes for a facial, so I think I should be able to do, er, *something* with your hair,' she finished, looking Pippa up and down the way she had the first time they had met.

Foo-Foo snarled and let out his trademark high-pitched, 'Yap, yappity-yap, yap!'

Pippa held Dash closer to her and whispered, 'Listen to what he says and let me know later.'

Trinity picked up one of Pippa's plaits and started

236

running it through her fingers as though it was made of something nasty and slimy. She grimaced. Then her eyes alighted on Dash, snuggled into Pippa's coat. She backed away at once, tears pricking in the corner of her eyes, her pointy nose turning pink at the end.

'Ask her what the matter is,' Dash hissed, glancing at the poodle. 'The pile of fluff's got nothing to say except, "Go away, you smell."'

Pippa nodded surreptitiously. 'W-what's the matter, Ms Meddler?' she asked.

'Nothing, nothing,' Trinity said, shaking her head and stepping back into her salon, her eyes streaming.

'Ask her again,' Dash insisted.

'Something has obviously upset you,' Pippa persisted, following Trinity into the building. For every step forward she took, Trinity took another two backwards.

'Yap, yappity-yap! Yap, yappity-yap!' Foo-Foo's accusations increased in volume.

Trinity fished for a hanky in her pocket and dabbed her face, then flapped it at Pippa, saying,

'Oh, I'm so sorry, my darling, it's just that your lovely little dog has reminded me of all the other dogs that have gone missing around here. I – I can't *bear* it.' Then she buried her face in her hanky and made a big show of blowing her nose very loudly (it was quite a disgusting noise and really rather rude).

'There's something fishy about this,' Dash was whispering. 'Trinity is not a woman to burst into tears like that. And anyway, she's got new customers out of the whole dog-disappearance episode.'

'Yap, yappity-yap!'

'Oh for crying out loud, will you shut up, you over-pampered powder puff!' barked Dash.

Pippa used the commotion as a cover to keep Trinity talking. 'Yes, I – I know what you mean, Ms Meddler. I have to say I'm really worried about Dash at the moment. I don't want *him* going missing too. That's why I brought him with me actually. I hope you don't mind if I bring him in while I have my hair done.'

Trinity looked utterly horrified now. By the look

 238

on her mucky, tear-stained, make-up-streaked face
you would think that Pippa had just asked if she
could bring a pet tarantula into the salon.

Pippa smiled encouragingly, and Dash made
himself look as wide-eyed, cute and appealing as
possible.

'Yap, yappity-yap!' Foo-Foo shrieked.

'Oh, Foo-Foo, darling, do be quiet. You're giving
Mummy the most awful nervous headache,' Trinity
twittered. She glanced wildly around the salon as
if looking for an escape route. Eventually, as Mrs
Fudge had predicted, the thought of losing out
on Pippa's custom seemed to get the better of her.
She stammered, 'Yes, no, of course you're worried
about your, er, lovely dog. But maybe you could
take him home first and then come back for your
appointment? I don't mind waiting a bit.'

Pippa felt the niggle of suspicion she had been
carrying around in the pit of her stomach grow into
a much more solid feeling of complete and utter
distrust. She narrowed her eyes.

Dash felt her tense up and muttered in warning, 'Don't let her think you're on to her.'

Pippa gave a tiny nod and then said to Trinity, 'I thought you said you only had half an hour free before Marble came for her face-change or whatever it was – good idea, that, actually . . . Anyway, I won't have time to go home and come back. Oh well,' she went on lightly, 'I suppose I don't need my hair done that much.'

Trinity's eyes flashed.

She really is too greedy to turn away an appointment, Pippa thought gleefully. I've got her now.

'No, you come in. Of course your little dog can stay,' she said. 'I'll put Foo-Foo out the back so that they don't fight.'

'Hah! Bad luck, fluffball!' Dash said with relish as the poodle was dragged kicking, scratching and yapping out of the salon.

'Listen, Dash,' Pippa said urgently the minute Trinity was out of earshot. 'Wait until I've got her

 240

talking, then you nip out and find Foo-Foo. I reckon that poodle must have some information – even if his brain is full of fluff.'

'I'll do my best,' agreed Dash.

When Trinity came back she looked genuinely upset, with red-rimmed eyes and tears still shining in the corners of her eyes. She made a palaver out of settling Dash on a cushion in the corner, sniffing woefully as she did so. Then, when Pippa pointed out that time was moving on, she grabbed a tray of bobbles and hair-ties and set to work, combing back Pippa's hair so tightly the poor girl had to speak through gritted teeth.

'It's amazing that you know where to get so many poodles from,' she gushed.

Dash quietly slipped out of the room.

'In fact, it's *very* clever of you,' Pippa went on. 'Are they expensive? We've never had a poodle in Crumbly-under-Edge before. I wouldn't really have

the faintest idea where to find so many of them. And
all so alike.'

Trinity narrowed her eyes at Pippa's reflection,
but when the little girl stared back, all wide-eyed
innocence, she relaxed and said smoothly, 'Oh, it's
just a case of knowing the right people. You know,
when my dear customers lost their pups and came to
tell me all about it, it did upset me so. It's the least I
can do to help them make up for their loss.'

'I wonder, being as clever as you are, perhaps you might have an idea where the other dogs have got to? Only, it's such a small town, and it does seem strange that so many dogs have vanished into thin air.'

Trinity yanked at a section of hair viciously and said, 'Dear me, is that the time? I'm afraid that's going to have to be all for today, Pippa darling. I must get ready for Marble. Now let's get your coat. I forgot I need to feed Foo-Foo before Marble arrives.'

Pippa checked swiftly around the salon and was relieved to see that Dash had magically returned to his cushion and was curled up as if asleep.

'Thank you for doing my hair,' Pippa said, trying hard to sound as if she meant it (which was difficult, as Trinity had broken off midway through braiding her hair, leaving her looking like half startled porcupine, half normal girl.)

Poor Pippa paid for her disastrous half a hairstyle and, calling for Dash to follow, scampered down the steps to her skateboard, cramming her hat on to cover her unfortunate new image.

243

'Did you find anything out?' Pippa asked as they whizzed along.

'Nothing definite, but the cinnamon perfume is absolutely Trinity's. The only problem with that is that everyone who goes to the salon smells of it these days.' He sniffed the air. 'In fact, I'm sorry to say, but *you* smell of it now.'

'Thanks,' Pippa said sarcastically.

'But I did smell something else – something that reminded me of our dear Mrs Fudge, actually.' His tail was whirring round and round. 'It's very faint, but I think it's that minty shampoo she used on Snooks the last time he came – do you remember?'

'Oh, Dash,' Pippa said sadly. 'It's a salon! Of course it smells of shampoo.' She was starting to feel more than a little disappointed by Dash's famous nose.

'Yes, but this was definitely the same shampoo Mrs Fudge uses, not one of those ultra-whiffy pongy poodly ones Trinity favours. And there's something else,' he added in a more sinister tone.

 244

'Yes?'

'There were traces of fur on the ground which I followed in a trail to the sheds in the back yard.'

'Poodle fur?' asked Pippa.

'No, that was the weird thing. It was the same colour as Snooks.' He paused.

Pippa stared at him.

'And George's and Winston's and pretty much any other kind of dog fur you care to imagine,' Dash finished in a hushed voice.

'OK,' said Pippa slowly. 'So what are you saying?'

'I am saying once and for all that our Ms Meddler knows more about the whereabouts of the lost pooches than she is letting on.' He paused and looked Pippa earnestly in the eyes. 'I am saying that she has dog-napped them!'

22

Lost and Found

'We need Raphael,' Pippa said later, when she and Dash were back at Mrs Fudge's.

Mrs Fudge was carefully sorting out Pippa's hair, restoring it to its normal state and gently brushing out the horrible tight braiding that Trinity had started. It hurt like the blazes of course, but Pippa could hardly go around looking like half porcupine, half ten-and-a-quarter-year-old girl, could she?

'I agree, dear. This sounds serious. He was here earlier, but I'll give him a call and ask him to come back when he's finished work.'

The postie turned up at the end of the day and Pippa filled him in on the morning's findings.

'The fur is not good news,' he said seriously, shaking his head. 'I tell you one ting, my darlin's: I seen that woman today, she keep a-coming and a-goin' from the back o' her salon an' *every time she come out* she has tears in her eyes, just like you tell me. I tink I have to in-vest-i-gate out the back, sweetheart. There be someting mighty suspicious out dere.' Raphael rapped his fingers on the kitchen table thoughtfully. 'I know! I can say I have a delivery of new shampoos and perfumes and creams for her and I need to carry them for her because they is sooooo heavy,' he said, a mischievous look on his face.

'Won't she think that's a bit odd if she hasn't put in an order?' Mrs Fudge pointed out. 'Raphael dear, what if you caused some other diversion while Dash nipped around the back? If Trinity is keeping the dogs somewhere in her salon, he will be bound to sniff them out, given enough time.'

'Great idea! So, Raphael – what will you do to distract Trinity?' asked Pippa.

Raphael's forehead creased in concentration. Then

his expression brightened and he said, 'How's about I flatter the old trout, eh?'

Pippa laughed. 'I'd love to see that!'

Raphael beamed. 'I tink it would be heasy-peasy to charm that silly vain woman. First, I get her attention by sayin' how beee-oo-tiful she is.' (He ignored Pippa doing her I'm-going-to-be-sick face.) 'Den I ask her , "How is you managin' to stay soooo young-lookin'?" Ha! She will be putty in my hands, sweetness!'

'It's true,' Dash agreed. 'I can just see her becoming so engrossed in talking about herself that she won't notice little old me slip in.'

The dachshund became very animated at the idea and sprang on to Mrs Fudge's lap, knocking Muffles flying. 'Have you any of your delicious dog biscuits left, Mrs Fudge?' he asked. 'If so, allow me to take some with me. If they don't tempt your old canine friends into kicking up a hoo-ha from their place of hiding, I don't know what will.'

★

And so the next morning, Pippa and Dash set off on Pippa's skateboard, closely following Raphael on his Rollerblades. The postie knocked on the door of the salon and immediately started his charm offensive.

'Good mornin' to you, Trinity my sweetness! And what a vision you are today. Is that a new necklace? And what have you done to your hair? You are truly an angel. No wonder your salon is called Heaven on Earth, darlin'!'

(No doubt *you* are probably making I'm-going-to-be-sick faces yourself at this point. I certainly am.)

As he wittered on Trinity blushed and asked him in for a chat. Dash and Pippa seized their moment and skittered through the salon straight to the back, Dash with a small bag of Mrs Fudge's treats in his mouth. Pippa went to the bottom of the yard and hid behind the big rubbish bins.

'I will lay the treats out around the yard,' Dash had told her earlier, 'and wait to see if anyone takes the bait. In the meantime, you stay hidden, ready to pounce if I need you.'

'Why do I have to hide?' Pippa had complained.

'Because,' Dash had said with increasing impatience, 'if Trinity comes out the back for any reason, a little dog sniffing around on his own will not look as suspicious as a skinny girl with long red hair and a little dog sniffing around together. Besides,' he finished, 'while I am being chased, you can make a run for it, unnoticed.'

So you see they had an excellent plan in place.

But then something happened that was not part of the plan at all. While Raphael and Trinity were deep in conversation, and while Pippa was hiding and Dash was sniffing and dropping the dog treats around the yard, a strange van pulled up by the back gate. In the front of the van were two men in some kind of uniform. They checked something on a piece of paper, nodded to each other and the man in the passenger seat got out. He was carrying a huge net and a nasty-looking stick.

But it was the two words written on the side of the van in fearsome black letters that frightened

Pippa most of all. Her mouth went dry and she stopped breathing as she read the  words aloud in a hoarse, terrified whisper:

'DOG CATCHERS!'

The human brain and the human body can be the most marvellous team. But there are times when they just do not want to work together, rather like those scenes in nightmares where your brain is shouting at your legs to run even faster than that time you won the two hundred metres last year at sports day, but your legs are saying sleepily that they would prefer to have forty winks just now instead, thank you very much.

Pippa's brain and body were having exactly that sort of disagreement just as the dog catcher was picking up the padlock on the back gates of Heaven on Earth. He seemed to know the code to unlock it, which was odd. The gates swung open and the man beckoned to the driver of the van to reverse in. The man then opened the back doors of the van and Pippa saw the interior was . . . one big cage.

A prison on wheels.

A prison for dogs!

Just when Pippa's legs were thinking they might after all pay attention to the screaming and hollering of her brain and actually move some time soon, lots of things happened at once.

The man who had unlocked the gates spotted Dash, who was dropping dog biscuits in a line around the outside of the sheds in the yard; Dash spotted the man and set off a cacophony of barking fit to wake a very dead person; the man shouted over the noise of the barking, 'I've got one of the little beggars!' and came charging towards Dash with his net held over his head.

Pippa screamed, 'Watch it, Dash!' and leaped out from behind the bins, sending them toppling over

and knocking into the other man, who had squeezed down the side of the van in response to his colleague. Dash hurtled at lightning speed towards the man with the net and bit him on the ankle, whereupon the man dropped his net and howled in pain.

The commotion had brought Raphael and Trinity out of the salon. Raphael was booming, 'What is de meanin' o' dis?' while the bitten dog catcher was cursing and shouting, 'You'll pay for this, Ms Meddler. You told us the place'd be deserted.'

As if this wasn't enough chaos, the noise level was suddenly increased by a chorus of barking from one of the sheds.

'It's all right!' Dash yapped, running to the door. 'Help is at hand! Pippa, ask Raphael to get the key from Trinity.'

But Raphael had already frogmarched Trinity to the door of the shed and was making her open it. She took a key from a chain around her waist and with shaking fingers turned it in the lock.

The lock was released, and Raphael jumped back

just in time as a whirlwind of barking and yapping and teeth and slobbery jaws rushed out of the shed and into the yard. George, Snooks and Winston were at the front of the stampede, closely followed by their friends and neighbours who had also gone missing in recent days.

Dash leaped over the fallen bins and flew with one final bound on to the roof of the dog catchers' van, where, in his loudest, most high-pitched bark, he called for 'SILENCE!'

The hullabaloo ceased immediately, and all the dogs turned to look up at him. He barked out a series of commands to the throng beneath him. In response, the dogs herded the men and Trinity into the back of the van, and Raphael and Pippa shut the doors on them. Then Pippa squeezed round to the front of the van and got the keys. She threw them up to Dash, who caught them in his mouth, and with a flick of his head threw them to Raphael, who used them to lock the doors to the van so that no one could escape. Then Dash leaped down and ran to Pippa.

She cradled him in her arms and nuzzled her button nose against his silky red fur. 'You are a superhero, Dash,' she said. 'I'm sorry I ever doubted you. In fact, you are a dog in a million.'

And all the other dogs barked in agreement.

The Bit at the End Where Everything Is Explained

Things were gradually returning to a version of normality in Crumbly-under-Edge now that Trinity Meddler had gone. People were shedding their ridiculous outfits and layers of make-up and starting to look a bit more like their old selves. The angels over the doorway of Heaven on Earth began to look shabby, the glitz and glamour of the place fading quickly. In contrast, the little blue and pink and green and creamy white houses were peaceful and bright in the late-autumn sunshine and everyone was happy that the dreadful storms and showers had at last gone away.

Mrs Fudge was very busy now that everyone had reclaimed their dogs. The poor creatures were in a

dreadful state from being locked up for so long, and they were desperately in need of a good shampoo. The pooch-pampering parlour was a humming hive of activity, and if you had been walking by the window and peeped in, you would have thought that nothing out of the ordinary had ever happened in the small town. (Mind you, Pippa Peppercorn's parents had never noticed anything unusual in the first place. They were still sitting at the kitchen table reading books and newspapers the last time I looked.)

'Mrs Fudge should re-open Chop 'n' Chat now too, don't you think, Raphael?' Pippa said happily. She had come straight from school and was sitting on the counter swinging her legs back and forth while she sucked on a cherry-fizz lollipop.

Raphael nodded, his postie's hat jauntily slipping down over one eye. 'You could take a leaf out o' that woman's book and do hairdressin' and dog groomin' at de same time!'

'I don't know,' said Mrs Fudge. She was brushing

poor Snooks's fur, getting rid of the last of the dust and muck. 'I'm quite busy enough with all these adorable pooches for now.'

Muffles gave a half-hearted snarl.

'Please do,' said Marble, looking up from *Terrier Times*. (She had decided not to look at magazines about Jollywood actresses – or indeed poodles – from now on, and was learning instead about how to best care for her lovely Welsh terrier.)

Pippa nearly choked on her lolly. She had never heard Marble say 'please' before.

'We are all so sorry we were taken in by that dreadful woman,' chipped in Coral, who was waiting on the sofa with Winston on her lap. He was looking as sorry for himself as Snooks – the folds of his soft fur were caked with dirt and his claws were long and scratchy.

'We should have known something was wrong,' agreed Mrs Prim, stroking George's knotted and scraggly coat. 'She was allergic to our lovely pooches, you know; that's what all the tears were about.'

259

'Yes,' said Mrs Fudge. 'I heard that was her excuse for kidnapping your dogs. She wanted you all to visit Heaven on Earth, but without your dogs.'

'I don't understand,' said Pippa. 'I mean, she had Foo-Foo, and she was the one who encouraged you to get your poodles too.'

'Poodles don't cause allergies,' said Marble knowledgeably. 'Their fur is different. It's more like wool apparently. That's why she wanted us all to replace our pets.'

'Kind of creepy though. Talking of poodles . . . You are – you are keeping your new pets too, aren't you?' Pippa asked anxiously. The thought of more animals being mistreated was too horrible to contemplate.

'I'm keeping mine,' said Coral, patting a small white head that was peeping out of her handbag. 'If Winston doesn't mind, that is. And if Mrs Fudge doesn't mind me bringing him in for a spot of pampering now and again.'

Winston barked and wagged his tail. The poodle gave a happy yappy bark in agreement.

Marble looked at Mrs Prim and she nodded. 'We'll keep ours too. It doesn't seem fair to punish the poor dogs for what Trinity has done.' Her poodle leaned out of her shopping basket and licked her hand.

Marble coughed embarrassedly. 'We would be as bad as Trinity if we abandoned them,' she added, shooting a loving look at both her dogs.

Pippa and Raphael exchanged a glance which seemed to say, 'Well, I never. Marble thinking of someone other than herself!'

Dash jumped up on to one of the twirly-whirly chairs and addressed the room (not caring that there were those in it who did not understand him).

'I for one welcome the poodles to Crumbly-under-Edge,' he announced. 'We canines must stick together.'

Snooks, Winston and George barked in agreement and the poodles yapped along merrily.

'Even . . .' Dash added archly, 'even if some of us *do* have fluff for brains.'

This story was written by a lady called **Anna Wilson**. She lives in a town which is rather like Crumbly-under-Edge, where there is a hair salon a bit like Mrs Fudge's: the ladies there are just as lovely as Mrs Fudge (although not as old) and they love to eat cake. **Anna** has two cats, Jet and Inky, who are quite like Muffles (except they are black), and a pooch called Kenna (who doesn't actually like being pampered, unless it involves food). She also has three chickens who lay eggs that are perfect for cake-baking. Titch, one of the chickens, quite likes being pampered. **Anna** is thinking of setting up a Poultry Pampering Parlour just for her.

If you would like to find out more about **Anna** and her books you can visit www.annawilson.co.uk. Or you can write to her:

Anna Wilson
c/o Macmillan Children's Books
20 New Wharf Road
London
N1 9RR

Anna would love to see your pet photos too! But don't forget to enclose a stamped addressed envelope if you want her to return them to you.

Monkey Business

Anna Wilson

It's so BORING having normal pets!

For Felix and Flo, animals are the NUMBER ONE
TOP PRIORITY in life. And although Felix loves
his pets (a lazy dog, an angry cat and a noisy hamster),
what he really wants is to look after an animal which
is EXOTIC and DIFFERENT. Will Flo's brilliant
and FOOLPROOF plan get Felix his perfect pet –
or will it just send him bananas?

A side-splittingly chaotic story about schemes,
dreams and monkeying around.

A selected list of titles available from Macmillan Children's Books

The prices shown below are correct at the time of going to press. However, Macmillan Publishers reserves the right to show new retail prices on covers, which may differ from those previously advertised.

All Pan Macmillan titles can be ordered from our website, www.panmacmillan.com, or from your local bookshop and are also available by post from:

Bookpost, PO Box 29, Douglas, Isle of Man IM99 1BQ

Credit cards accepted. For details:
Telephone: 01624 677237
Fax: 01624 670923
Email: bookshop@enterprise.net
www.bookpost.co.uk

Free postage and packing in the United Kingdom